Dear Diary,

Always a bride~~smaid~~... I never used to really think that old adage might turn out to be true for me. Though I have to admit, being a bridesmaid is an honor and a lot of fun, especially since it's for my good friend Hannah.

Alexandra and I spent the day with Hannah and her wedding planner, Dana Ulrich, at the Smith Tower. Carlos, my mischievous foster son, insisted that I sit in the Wishing Chair. He'd heard the legend that if a woman sits in the chair, she'll marry within the year. I guess he's also worried I'll end up single!

I felt a bit embarrassed, but to please Carlos I sat in the chair. Luckily Dana is a good sport and she agreed to have a turn, too. I have a feeling her prospects are better than mine. Hannah told me that Jack's half brother, Austin Hawke, is helping Dana with the wedding arrangements. And since Hannah and Jack's houseboat is a little crowded, Austin's staying at Dana's place. Hmm...possibilities?

Seems to me that it might take more than a Wishing Chair to get those two together, though. Dana's dreams of planning perfect weddings for Seattle brides and Austin's dreams of raising cattle on his Texas ranch don't exactly mesh. Still, I can look on the bright side. It's a million-to-one chance, but if the Wishing Chair does work its magic for this unlikely twosome, maybe there's hope for me!

Till tomorrow, Katherine

SUPER ROMANCE

Two-time RITA® Award winner **Kristin Gabriel**
lives on a farm in central Nebraska with her husband,
children, a springer spaniel and assorted cats. She
is the author of almost twenty books for Harlequin;
her first novel, *Bullets over Boise,* was turned into a
made-for-television movie called *Recipe for Revenge.*
Kristin met her husband in college, then made
the bumpy transition from city girl to farm wife,
providing plenty of fodder for her stories. A busy
mom with three active teenagers, Kristin divides
her time between writing and attending school
activities. Her hobbies include reading, dieting
and procrastination. Kristin enjoys hearing
from her readers and can be reached through
her Web site at www.KristinGabriel.com.

Forrester Square

LEGACIES . LIES . LOVE .

KRISTIN GABRIEL
THIRD TIME'S THE CHARM

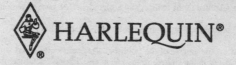

HARLEQUIN®

TORONTO • NEW YORK • LONDON
AMSTERDAM • PARIS • SYDNEY • HAMBURG
STOCKHOLM • ATHENS • TOKYO • MILAN • MADRID
PRAGUE • WARSAW • BUDAPEST • AUCKLAND

HARLEQUIN BOOKS
225 Duncan Mill Road, Don Mills,
Ontario, Canada M3B 3K9

ISBN 0-373-61274-5

THIRD TIME'S THE CHARM

Kristin Gabriel is acknowledged as the author of this work.

Visit us at www.eHarlequin.com

Printed in U.S.A.

Dear Reader,

I love weddings, so it seems only natural to write a story about a wedding planner. One of the best-kept secrets of the industry is that no wedding is perfect. There are always a few glitches along the way. Even couples who spend months planning that perfect day can't predict everything that might happen. I've heard stories of bridezillas terrorizing everyone in their path (including the groom), attendants fainting at the altar, caterers who run out of food at the reception, and even thieves stealing all the wedding gifts.

In *Third Time's the Charm,* wedding planner Dana Ulrich's problem is a cowboy who teams up with her to plan his brother's wedding. Austin Hawke knows nothing about weddings and even less about city girls, but that doesn't stop him from trying to romance her all the way to the altar!

I hope you enjoy this addition to the Forrester Square continuity series.

Happy reading,

Kristin Gabriel

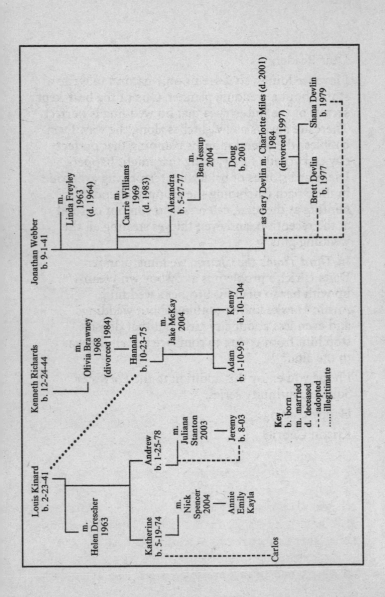

Louis Kinard
b. 2-23-41
m.
Helen Drescher
1963

Kenneth Richards
b. 12-24-44
m.
Olivia Brawney 1968
(divorced 1984)

Jonathan Webber
b. 9-1-41
m.
Linda Freyley
1963
(d. 1964)
m.
Carrie Williams
1969
(d. 1983)

Katherine
b. 5-19-74
m.
Nick Spencer
2004

Andrew
b. 1-25-78
m.
Juliana Stanton
2003

Hannah
b. 10-23-75
m.
Jake McKay
2004

Alexandra
b. 5-27-77
m.
Ben Jessup
2004

as Gary Devlin m. Charlotte Miles (d. 2001)
1984
(divorced 1997)

Annie
Emily
Kayla

Jeremy
b. 8-03

Adam
b. 1-10-95

Kenny
b. 10-1-04

Doug
b. 2001

Brett Devlin
b. 1977

Shana Devlin
b. 1979

Carlos

Key
b. born
m. married
d. deceased
- - - deceased
......illegitimate

CHAPTER ONE

AUSTIN HAWKE SAW his half brother standing at the end of the long, narrow dock. His first impulse was to punch Jack McKay in the nose. The second was to turn around and go back to Texas. But he'd already come too far, all the way to Seattle, to turn back now.

Jack had changed a lot in the past ten years. No longer a renegade cowboy, he'd cut his shaggy black hair and exchanged his jeans and snakeskin boots for a pair of khaki slacks and leather Top-Siders. His big brother even wore a tie.

But time couldn't straighten the nose that had been broken in a bar fight all those years ago. Or erase the scar below his left eye. Maybe Jack could put the past behind him, but they both carried scars from growing up on the Hawke Ranch together.

Austin paused, just watching. Jack hadn't seen him yet; his attention was on the woman standing at his side. Hannah Richards.

Austin hadn't seen her since she was a college coed in Dallas. Golden highlights shimmered in her hair as the sun skimmed the waters of Lake Union. She and Jack held hands, their bodies lightly brushing against each other as they watched the fading sunset.

He knew Jack would be surprised to see him. Just as Austin had been surprised a week ago when Jack called him after almost ten years of silence. He still wasn't sure what had prompted it. Their telephone call had been short and stilted—the first words spoken between them since Jack left Texas a decade ago.

In that phone call, Austin had learned that Jack and Hannah were planning to marry. And that he had a nephew, Adam McKay. Jack and Hannah's son. A boy who had lived his first nine years without a mother.

Thanks to me.

A twinge of guilt gnawed at the pit of his stomach. Jack might not blame Austin for tearing his family apart all those years ago, but Austin couldn't see it any other way. Now the only question was whether Jack would wreak revenge.

He had the perfect weapon to do it—though he wasn't aware of it yet.

Austin inhaled a deep breath of salty, damp air as he started toward them again, the loud *clump* of his cowboy boots on the dock announcing his presence.

Hannah glanced over at him, then looked again, her light blue eyes widening in sudden recognition.

"Austin?" she gasped.

Jack turned around, his jaw sagging when he saw his brother in front of him.

"Howdy," Austin said, tipping up his hat.

Jack narrowed his eyes. "This is a hell of a surprise, Austin. When did you get into town?"

"I just drove in today."

"Why didn't you tell me you were coming?"

Austin met his brother's gaze. "I wasn't sure I'd be welcome."

"You're family," Hannah said, glancing up at Jack. "You'll always be welcome here."

Something hard lodged in his throat and he tried to remember the last time he'd felt like part of a family. Jack had left home ten years ago without so much as a goodbye. Austin, barely eighteen, had taken off shortly after that, not willing to handle his drunken father on his own.

He'd drifted from job to job, honing his skills as a ranch hand on some of the biggest spreads in Texas. But he'd never really belonged anywhere.

Just like he didn't belong in Seattle. He'd come up here to deliver a message, plain and simple. Only, Hannah's warm welcome threw him off balance, and he struggled to find the words he needed to say.

Austin turned his gaze to the yellow house that sat on pilings in the water beside the dock. "So, you really live here?"

"That's right," Jack said, sizing up the brother he hadn't seen for a decade.

"I moved in a few weeks ago," Hannah added. "I never thought I'd find myself living on a houseboat, but it's been fun. And it's made the adjustment easier on Adam."

Austin looked at the two of them, wondering how they had ever managed to find each other again. He could remember their hot and heavy romance back in Texas. Hannah had been a shy college student then, while Jack had preferred to spend his time in Dallas honky-tonks.

"How about something to drink?" Hannah offered, turning toward the house. "I've got some ice-cold beer in the refrigerator."

"Maybe later," Austin replied, ready to deliver the

news he'd traveled over two thousand miles to give.
"I need to talk to Jack first."

Hannah took the cue. "Why don't you two stay out
here and talk, while I go inside and get dinner ready?"
Then she looked up at Austin. "I hope you'll join us."

He hesitated. "I don't want you to go to any trouble."

"It's no trouble," Hannah assured him. "I put a
chuck roast in the slow cooker this morning, so all I
have to do is dish it up. Adam is staying overnight
with a friend, so it will just be the three of us."

Then she smiled up at him. "And don't worry about
your stomach, either. I'm a much better cook than I
was ten years ago."

Austin's mouth twitched at the memory of the
banana-cream pie she'd once baked for his big brother.
Even their Border collie, Rusty, had turned up his nose
at it.

"Thanks, Hannah," he replied, wondering if he'd
still be welcome by the time he and Jack were done
talking. "I appreciate the invitation."

"Then, I'll set another plate." She rounded the pic-
nic table and headed toward the floating houseboat.
"Dinner should be ready in about fifteen minutes."

Austin saw Jack's gaze follow his fiancée until she
disappeared through the front door.

"Hannah hasn't changed much."

Jack turned back to him. "You'd be surprised."
Then he folded his arms across his chest. "I never
thought I'd see you in Seattle, Austin. What brings you
here?"

"The old man is dead." Austin hadn't meant to

blurt out the news, but he hadn't known how else to say it.

He watched a shadow cross Jack's face, then saw him slowly nod.

"So, that's why you came."

"It's one reason."

Jack took a deep breath. "What happened? Did somebody crack a bottle over his head? Or did he finally drink himself to death?"

"Neither one. He got pneumonia. Apparently, his body was too worn down by alcohol to fight it."

"Apparently?"

"I haven't seen the old man for years," Austin explained. "His attorney found me and gave me the news, since I was listed as the executor of his estate in the will."

An estate that consisted of the run-down Hawke Ranch and little else. Lincoln Hawke had sold practically everything he'd owned to pay his running tab at the Longhorn Bar, leaving only the land untouched. Even it had looked worn and tired to Austin's eyes, along with the house and barn. The ranch was almost beyond repair—just like his family.

"When did this happen?" Jack asked.

"About a month ago."

For a moment Jack didn't say anything. "So I guess I missed the funeral."

"There was no service," Austin replied. "The old man wanted it that way."

Jack turned and stared out over the water. "He was probably afraid nobody would show up."

"Probably."

Lincoln Hawke hadn't been a popular man, not even

at the Longhorn Bar, where he'd spent so much of his time. He'd been a mean drunk, something that both Jack and Austin had learned the hard way. Though he'd never physically abused either boy, he'd found other ways to hurt them. Pitting them against each other. Claiming they were no good.

It hadn't started out that way. Loretta McKay had been a widow with three-year-old Jack to care for, when she'd met and married Lincoln Hawke in a whirlwind romance. Austin was born a year later, and the family all got along well enough, eking out a decent living on the Hawke Ranch on the outskirts of Dallas.

But Loretta was killed in a car accident the day after Austin turned twelve years old. After her death, Linc began to spend more and more time at the bar and less time paying attention to his sons. Drunk more often than sober, Linc lashed out with verbal assaults, making it clear that neither one of the boys could ever please him.

Left to their own devices, twelve-year-old Austin and sixteen-year-old Jack grew to depend on each other. Austin had worshiped his older brother, eventually following him into one wild scrape after another. They grew up to be the kind of bad boys that Texas mamas warn their daughters about, drawing both trouble and women like magnets.

The two of them had always faced the lonely world together—until one drunken summer night at a seedy Dallas honky-tonk. A night that had ripped them apart and kept them that way for the past ten years.

Jack turned to face Austin. "So, why didn't you tell me he was dead when I called last week?"

"I thought I should deliver the news in person. Although, I wasn't sure you'd care."

Jack's gaze hardened. "Did you care?"

"I gave up caring about anybody a long time ago." Austin knew that sounded harsh, but life was simply easier that way. People couldn't let you down if you didn't care about them. Austin had learned that he couldn't depend on anybody but himself.

"Then, I guess there's nothing more to say."

"Not quite," Austin replied. "According to the lawyer, the old man quit drinking about a month before he died. Maybe he knew his body couldn't handle it anymore. Or maybe he realized his time was almost up. Whatever the reason, he must have spent that month full of regret about the way he'd let the ranch go. About the way he'd let us go."

"Kicked me out is more accurate," Jack muttered.

"What do you mean?"

"I mean, Linc told me that both of you wanted me out of the house. Out of your lives."

His gut tightened. "And you believed him?"

"Hell, Austin, why shouldn't I have believed him?" He stroked his jaw. "Especially since you almost broke my jaw in that barroom brawl. You pack quite a punch, little brother. I taught you well."

Austin still remembered that night. How he'd walked into the bar to see his girl in Jack's arms. That's when he'd decked him. Then another cowboy had swung on him, and before he knew it, the whole place had erupted into a brawl. Austin had barely been able to walk by the time he'd grabbed his girl and hustled her out of the bar.

He'd never seen his brother again—until today. Jack

had been hauled off to jail for a few days; then, after his release, he left Dallas without a word. His abandonment had hurt Austin more than his girlfriend's betrayal or the three broken ribs he'd suffered in the brawl.

Jack snorted. "I still can't believe you thought I was moving in on your girl. She came on to me. Casey Morningstar was the biggest flirt east of Dallas."

"I finally figured that out when she left me for a bull rider from Laredo," Austin said wryly.

"You were as blind as a lovesick bull back then," Jack replied. "And twice as stubborn."

"Stubborn enough to believe the old man when he told me that you'd taken off because you'd had it with both of us."

Jack nodded. "That sounds like the old man. Playing us against each other was his specialty."

Austin couldn't argue with that—especially when he knew that Linc had gotten in one last power play before his death.

"How about that beer?" Jack offered, moving toward the houseboat.

"All right." Austin had more to tell him, but washing down the rest of it with a beer might make it more palatable. He followed his brother through the front door of the houseboat, finding it small but surprisingly cozy inside.

A huge floor-to-ceiling window took up one entire wall, providing a picture-perfect view of Lake Union. The last rays of twilight reflected off the surface of the lake and splashed a rainbow of colors onto one wall of the living room.

Though Austin stood on a solid hardwood floor, the

house swayed ever so slightly on the water, making him feel a little off balance. Or maybe it was seeing Jack again. The awkwardness between them made him regret accepting the dinner invitation. But what did he expect after everything that had happened?

"Have a seat," Jack said as he headed toward the kitchen.

Austin could see Hannah standing in front of the stove, stirring one of the pots. The savory aroma of roast beef in the air made his mouth water and reminded him how little he'd eaten since he'd seen Texas in his rearview mirror.

"Here you go," Jack said, tossing him a cold bottle from the refrigerator.

"Thanks." Austin caught the beer and seated himself on one of the chairs at the kitchen table.

Jack joined him there, twisting the cap off another bottle before offering it to Hannah. "Care to join us?"

"No, thanks," she said, grimacing slightly. "My stomach's been a little upset today. That's the downside of running a day-care center. You're exposed to every virus that comes through the place."

Austin looked up in surprise. "You run a day-care center?"

Hannah nodded. "With my two old friends, Katherine Kinard and Alexandra Webber. We spent a large part of our childhood together in a neighborhood called Forrester Square in the Queen Anne district. So we decided to name our business Forrester Square Day Care, even though it's located in the Belltown district. We all love it, but it certainly keeps us busy."

"Too busy." Jack gave her a worried frown. "You haven't been feeling well for weeks, Hannah. I think you're trying to do too much. Not only work, but trying to plan our wedding in two short months.''

Hannah smiled as she carefully removed the roast from the slow cooker. ''You didn't even want to wait that long, remember? Besides, I won't have to do much of anything now that I've hired a wedding planner.''

''You did what?'' Jack set his bottle down on the table. ''When?''

''I met with Dana Ulrich this morning and we just clicked,'' Hannah replied. ''She's got some great ideas and she comes cheap. So I gave her the job.''

''Dana Ulrich,'' Jack said slowly. ''Isn't she the woman they call the—''

''Don't say it.'' Hannah held up one hand. ''It might be bad luck.''

''*She's* the bad luck,'' Jack replied. ''At least, according to *Seattle Magazine*.''

''That article was a hit job.'' Hannah pulled three plates out of the cupboard. ''Anyone can look bad if you twist the facts in the story.''

''What is the story?'' Austin asked, bringing the beer bottle to his lips.

''This Ulrich woman botched the last two weddings on her docket,'' Jack said with a scowl.

''It wasn't her fault,'' Hannah countered. ''I know how tough it is to start a new business. I'm sure all that negative publicity didn't help her.''

''Negative publicity?'' Austin echoed.

Jack turned to his brother. ''My fiancée just hired a wedding planner whose last two brides bolted before the ceremony.''

"Don't worry, Jack," she teased. "I'm not letting you get away this time."

Her words made Austin's gut tense. He took the platter Hannah handed him and stabbed a slice of the juicy beef, knowing he wouldn't be able to swallow a bite until he confessed his role in their estrangement.

"It was partly my fault he got away the first time," Austin admitted.

Jack looked up him, his brow furrowed. "What do you mean?"

Austin set down his fork, knowing he might very well be asked to leave their home by the time he was done. "I'm talking about a phone call Hannah made almost ten years ago to the Hawke Ranch, looking for Jack. The old man answered, and she told him that it was urgent."

Hannah nodded. "My father had been in a horrible car accident and I had to fly to Seattle before I could tell Jack what happened. It was touch and go for a while. We didn't know if he was going to make it."

Austin could feel Jack's hard gaze on him. "I overheard the two of you on the extension while I was laid up in bed after that bar fight—still mad as hell that Jack had been kissing my girl in that honky-tonk."

"That girl was just grateful because I'd rescued her from a cowboy who got a little too friendly," Jack said, glancing at Hannah.

"No." Austin shook his head. "Casey was in love with you. Hell, Jack, all the women were in love with you. I was just young and stupid and jealous as hell."

"That was all a long time ago," Hannah said, obviously ready to change the subject. "What does it matter now?"

"It matters because I overheard that phone call you had with the old man," Austin told her. "He was drunk, as usual, and I knew Jack was in jail and would never get your message unless I gave it to him." He sucked in a deep breath. "But I never did."

A muscle flexed in Jack's jaw, but he didn't say a word.

"You're not to blame." Hannah glanced back and forth at the two of them. "We all made mistakes."

"Only, you and Jack both paid for my mistake," Austin said, not willing to whitewash his part in it. "So did your son."

Austin hadn't known that Hannah was pregnant at the time of that phone call. She'd ultimately given up her baby for adoption, believing Jack didn't want either one of them when he never returned any of the messages she'd left with Lincoln Hawke. She didn't know until this year that Jack had been contacted about relinquishing his parental rights and had decided to take Adam and raise the baby himself.

"It's too late to change the past," Jack snapped. "I never got the message. Linc just kicked me out of the house, telling me neither one of you wanted to see me again."

"I never knew that until today," Austin replied, hoping he would have been honorable enough to put an end to that lie if he had known about it. But he couldn't be sure. Nursing a broken heart as well as three broken ribs, he had been bitterly hurt over his girlfriend's betrayal as only an eighteen-year-old can be.

"All I knew was that you packed up and moved out without a word to me," Austin continued. "The old man said you were ashamed of us. Since I'd started the fight that landed you in jail, I thought it was true.''

''And since I still had the sore jaw you'd given me the night before,'' Jack replied, ''I guess I believed him when he said you wanted me to go.''

''Which just proves that foolishness is genetic,'' Hannah quipped. ''Fortunately, Adam has more sense than the two of you put together—though I've seen glimpses of the same stubborn pride. I can't believe you let Lincoln Hawke's lies keep you two apart for this long.''

Austin stared at her. ''You're not angry?''

''Of course I'm angry,'' Hannah retorted. ''But I'm angry at the man who is really responsible. Lincoln Hawke played games with all of our lives and probably took pleasure in the trouble and turmoil he caused each one of us. He's the reason you two haven't spoken to each other for ten years. I just wish there was some way to make him pay for it.''

''You can stop wishing, honey,'' Jack said. ''The man is dead. And I can't say I'm sorry, since he never did a damn thing for me.''

Hannah blinked. ''Dead?''

''It's true,'' Austin told her, ready to lay it all out on the table. ''And according to his lawyer, the old man came to regret the way he'd treated Jack. In fact, he even tried to make up for it.''

''How?'' Hannah asked, seating herself on a chair next to her fiancé.

''He left half the ranch to Jack.''

Two forks clattered onto the table, and both Hannah and Jack stared at him.

''You've got to be kidding,'' Jack said.

"Nope." Austin stabbed a piece of beef and raised it to his mouth. "Half of the Hawke Ranch is yours."

He didn't tell them about the plans he'd had to rebuild the place. The years he'd spent saving money so he could turn the ranch into a prosperous operation again. His father had always told him the ranch was his legacy. That it was Austin's job to return the place to its former glory. At the same time, Lincoln Hawke had expressed his doubts that Austin could do it.

Was that the reason he'd left half the ranch to Jack? Or was it simply one last chance to pit the brothers against each other? Austin didn't know the answer, but he had no doubt the old man was probably laughing in his grave at this moment.

"But that ranch has been in the Hawke family for over a hundred years," Jack told him. "It's your legacy—your birthright."

Austin chewed slowly, hoping he could say the words without the bitterness that had consumed him for the past month. He swallowed. "The will is legal and binding, Jack. You're the proud owner of five hundred acres of prime Texas grazing land."

"Jack is a parole officer now," Hannah said. "He's not interested in ranching anymore." She cast a curious glance at her fiancé. "Are you?"

Jack gave her hand a reassuring squeeze. "Of course not. My cowboy days were over a long time ago. My life is here with you and Adam."

Hannah looked relieved. "Then, we'll sell the land."

"Are you interested in buying?" Jack asked, turning to his brother.

"Look," Austin told him honestly. "I'll admit I want those acres...no, I *need* those acres to turn the place into a working ranch again. But I can't make you an offer. Not yet.''

"What's the problem?''

"I'm still waiting for the loan to come through. The old man didn't make a lot of friends at the bank, so the Hawke name isn't exactly high on their list of dependable borrowers.''

"The land should be enough collateral for a loan,'' Jack countered.

"It should,'' Austin agreed. "The loan officer just hasn't decided if I'm worth the risk.''

"When will you know?'' Hannah asked.

He shrugged. "A few more weeks. They're contacting my former employers for references and digging a little deeper into my background.''

"So we'll wait,'' his brother said.

Austin didn't want Jack doing him any favors. "The point is that there are plenty of cattlemen who would be itching to take that land off your hands for a lot more money than I can afford to pay right now. You should at least have it appraised. Talk to an attorney—''

"Hell, Austin,'' Jack interjected. "I don't really care what it's worth. I don't want the place. I don't want *anything* from Lincoln Hawke. As far as I'm concerned, you can have the land for free.''

His jaw tightened. "I don't take charity. Like it or not, half the ranch is yours, Jack.''

"Remember that stubborn pride I mentioned earlier,'' Hannah muttered under her breath.

"Well, I can be just as stubborn,'' Jack told her. "And I damn well intend to make sure the old man doesn't screw up Austin's life the way he tried to screw up mine.''

Both men knew too well how Lincoln Hawke's mind had worked, though Austin sensed Jack's anger had more to do with derailing Linc's final wishes than looking out for his little brother. They might be sharing a meal together, but there was still tension between them. The disappointment and distrust that had built up over a decade could not be torn down in one day.

"How do you intend to do that?" Austin asked.

"By drawing up a legal contract that satisfies us both. And the first condition will be that I'm willing to take payments on the land for the appraised value."

Austin shook his head. "I don't even know for sure if I'll qualify for a loan. You haven't been home for ten years, Jack. The ranch is so run-down, I doubt you'd even recognize it."

"Are you willing to make the payments?" Jack asked him.

"Yes, but I'm telling you that I don't know how long that will take. The first thing I have to do is rebuild the herd."

A puzzled frown crinkled Jack's brow. "What about the old man's herd?"

"He sold it eight years ago. Apparently, ranching interfered with his drinking, so he rented the grazing land to a neighbor and lived off the lease payments. Which means I'll have to start from scratch."

Jack considered that for a moment, then nodded. "I can live with that. I'll take whatever you can pay me whenever you can pay it."

"That's too generous," Austin argued. He'd already convinced himself that Jack would sell his share to someone else. That his dream of rebuilding the ranch would end before it could even start. "I want that contract to spell out the payments in black and white. With interest."

"Fine," Jack said. "Just promise me that you'll prove the old man wrong. Make the Hawke Ranch bigger and better than it's ever been before."

Austin's throat tightened. Jack had obviously overheard the old man voice doubts about his son's ability to take over the ranch. Jack knew the hell Austin had endured growing up with an alcoholic father, because he had endured that same hell. They might be strangers now, but they shared the same past.

"I intend to. First thing in the morning, I'm heading back for Texas."

"Wait," Hannah said, "I have another condition."

Both men looked at her. Caught up in memories of the past, Austin had almost forgotten she was there. But now uneasiness washed over him. He knew this had been too easy.

"What is it?" Jack asked.

She took a deep breath. "I want you to stay in Seattle until the wedding."

Austin frowned. "Why?"

"Because it's silly for you to turn right back around and go back to Texas after coming all this way. Because you and Jack haven't seen each other for ten years." She looked beseechingly at his brother for support, but Jack didn't say anything. Hannah turned back to Austin, obviously still searching for a convincing reason for him to stick around. "Because...we need you. We need you to help Dana Ulrich plan our wedding."

Austin stared at her, certain she had to be joking. But she looked alarmingly serious. *"Plan your wedding?"*

Jack frowned in concern, then laid his palm on her forehead. "I think you really are sick."

"I'm not sick," she assured him, taking his hand off her head and brushing a kiss across the back of his knuckles. "But you were right before, Jack. I really haven't been feeling well. Maybe I am trying to do too much. And you've got a full caseload at work."

"That's true," he agreed slowly.

"So, why don't we let Austin deal with all the small details of putting the wedding together? It's the perfect solution."

"Hold on a minute," Austin said, raising both hands in the air. He had to stop this runaway train before it ran completely off the tracks. "This is a very bad idea. I don't know anything about weddings. I don't *want* to know anything about weddings."

"But you know both of us," Hannah countered. "If you think the land deal Jack offered is too generous, then stay here and do us this favor. After that, we'll be even."

He hesitated. "What exactly would I have to do?"

"Just give us progress reports," Hannah replied, then turned to Jack. "This should solve any concerns you have about Dana Ulrich botching up our wedding."

Austin wanted to make sure he understood. "So you want me to stay in Seattle for the next two months?"

"Is that a problem?" Hannah asked, her smile fading. "Do you have a job waiting for you back in Texas?"

"No," he replied, still stunned by Hannah's condition. He wanted the Hawke Ranch more than anything in the world, but this was crazy. "I got laid off at the Double K after calving season."

"You could stay here with us," Hannah offered, trying her best to convince him. "It would give you and Jack a chance to get reacquainted. And I'm sure Adam would like to get to know his uncle Austin."

"And I'd like to meet him," Austin replied, realizing with a sudden pang that he really didn't have anywhere else to go. No one who needed him.

He'd been partially responsible for keeping these two apart. For letting Adam grow up without his mother. And now all she wanted from him was help planning their wedding.

Was that really too much to ask?

"So, will you do it?" she asked, hope lighting her blue eyes.

"That's up to Jack." He turned to his brother, who had remained strangely silent since hearing his fiancée's unusual condition. If Jack balked at the idea, then Austin was out of here. He wouldn't stay where he wasn't wanted.

Jack hesitated, then looked at Hannah. "If I agree, will you promise to make an appointment with the doctor next week for a physical?"

She gave him a solemn nod. "I promise."

"Then, I guess we've got a deal," Jack said, extending his hand.

Austin clasped it firmly in his own, knowing his brother probably didn't like the idea of their living together, even for two months, any more than he did. Despite their shared past and Hannah's hope for a full reconciliation, they were almost strangers now. They'd been apart too long to ever be a real family again.

But Austin still felt he owed them. And it was a debt he could repay by putting together the best damn Texas-style wedding Seattle had ever seen.

CHAPTER TWO

"I WANT MY TRADEMARK to be designing elegant and sophisticated weddings," Dana Ulrich said, all too aware of the small tape recorder on the coffee table between her and the reporter. She licked her dry lips, trying to sound cool and composed. Not desperate and destitute.

But thanks to that horrible feature article in last month's issue of *Seattle Magazine,* her business was hanging by a silk thread. All but one of her clients had dropped her cold. Apparently, few brides wanted the woman dubbed as the "wedding jinx" involved in the most important day of their lives.

So she'd been forced to spend most of her profits on an advertising blitz. The response had not been overwhelming. Only one person had called the number listed in the ads, and though Dana was grateful to have this new client, it was not enough to keep her business afloat.

She reached up to rub her temple with her fingertips. A small, throbbing ache indicated that another migraine might be on its way. A friend in nursing had suggested the headaches could be triggered by a poor diet. Dana knew she wasn't eating enough, but she'd skipped lunch again today—something that was becoming a bad habit with her.

"So, what kind of wedding would you envision for me?" Debbie North asked.

A reporter from the *Seattle Post-Intelligencer,* Debbie wore a hot-pink pantsuit with lipstick to match. In her late twenties, she was of average height and build, with her short brown hair the same shade as her eyes. An average American woman who wanted to be more than average.

Dana knew that feeling all too well. She'd grown up on the wrong side of the tracks in Seattle, fighting to fit in. To be somebody special. Without the money or means to attend college, she'd hired on as an assistant to Marco Kahn, a dress designer who specialized in bridal gowns. He'd become both her mentor and her friend, encouraging her to pursue her dream of starting her own business as a wedding planner. A dream that had recently turned into a nightmare.

"Let me think a minute," Dana said, considering the reporter's question. The woman's clothes suggested flash over style, but Debbie's questions were both intuitive and intelligent. She'd crave something unique, but with a touch of elegance.

"I see an outdoor wedding in the Cascades," Dana mused. "In early autumn, with the glorious fall colors in full array. Instead of the traditional white or ivory, your bridal gown might be a burnished gold silk. There would be a harpist providing the music, with the ceremony itself near a babbling mountain brook."

"That sounds absolutely perfect," the reporter said wistfully.

Dana smiled. "So, do I have a new client?"

Debbie laughed, shaking her head. "I'm too wrapped up in my career to make any time for romance. But how about you? Your career is all about romance. Does some of it overflow into your personal life?''

"I'm still waiting for Mr. Right to show up at my door,'' Dana hedged, not admitting she hadn't had a date for months. Impending bankruptcy tended to make you put men on the back burner. "I've seen too many couples who aren't perfect for each other to make that mistake.''

"Is that the reason the last two weddings you planned didn't work out?''

Dana glanced at the tape recorder.

Debbie leaned over to switch it off. "If you like, this part of the interview can be off the record.''

"That's what the freelance reporter for *Seattle Magazine* told me,'' Dana muttered. "Right before he tried to ruin my career.''

"That's the reason I'm here,'' Debbie told her. "The moment Hannah Richards pointed out that hatchet job to me, I decided to do this interview. I usually stick to investigative reporting, but I simply don't approve of that kind of attack journalism. Especially since that so-called reporter didn't disclose the fact that his sister was one of your competitors.''

"You know Hannah?'' Dana asked, surprised. She'd assumed the newspaper had sent a reporter here for a story after Dana had poured what was left of her life savings into an advertising blitz. Maybe she'd been wrong.

Debbie nodded. "I've been working on an old story involving Hannah's father, Kenneth Richards. He was a good friend and business partner of Louis Kinard, who was released from prison last fall after serving a twenty-year sentence for embezzlement.''

"I think I remember reading about his release in the newspaper a few months ago."

"I know it's an old story, but it still fascinates me," Debbie confided. "Kinard was also convicted of selling secrets from Eagle Aerotech, the business he owned with Richards and another friend, Jonathan Webber. But he's always maintained his innocence."

"Kinard and Webber," Dana mused. "Hannah's bridesmaids are Katherine Kinard and Alexandra Webber."

"The three of them recently opened Forrester Square Day Care together," Debbie said. "I just hope their business venture doesn't end as badly for them as it did for their fathers. Louis Kinard went to jail and Alexandra's parents were killed in a house fire around that same time. The poor girl was only six. I think that's one of the reasons this old story intrigues me so much. With the three of them opening Forrester Square Day Care, it's almost like history repeating itself."

"Yet you still made time for my story."

"Because it intrigues me, too," Debbie replied honestly. "I've done some research on you."

"Oh?" Dana stiffened.

"You overcame a tough childhood and now seem determined to make it on your own. You've got an up-and-coming business, not to mention this great apartment."

Dana just smiled, not bothering to divulge that the apartment was really her friend Marco's. He was in Paris working with one of the most prominent fashion designers in the world. But when the lease was up next month, Dana would be back out on the street—literally. That's why she had to turn her business around before it was too late.

It wouldn't be easy. Weddings were all about appearances—about making a lasting impression. Dana had to present herself the same way. Somehow she'd managed to serve her clients gourmet appetizers on a shoestring budget. She wore designer clothes bought cheap at secondhand stores and did her best to hide the fact that people used to call her poor white trash.

A fact that Debbie North had discovered with just a little digging.

"I'd prefer it if you'd leave my past out of the article," Dana said.

"But our readers eat up stories about people who have overcome the odds." She looked down at her notes. "According to my research, your father became seriously ill when you were a child, and your family had to go on public assistance so your mother could care for him. You never attended college, and worked two menial jobs for several years to help support your parents until your father's death three years ago." She glanced up at Dana. "Do I have it right so far?"

"Yes, but I'd really rather focus on the future," Dana said, amazed and a little uneasy to find out how much the reporter had discovered about her. She'd worked hard to create a new life for herself. To erase the old Dana Ulrich. "Like the upcoming Van Hoek wedding."

Debbie's eyes widened. "You've got that job?"

Dana nodded. "It should be the biggest society wedding this season."

"No kidding. So Alison Van Hoek wasn't scared away by the magazine article?"

"I don't think she reads much," Dana admitted. "We went to high school together and..." Her voice trailed off when she realized she was delving into the past again. Definitely a place she didn't want to go.

But Debbie smelled a story. "What a great angle for my article! Two old high school friends reunite to put on the biggest wedding extravaganza of the season."

"We weren't exactly friends," Dana demurred.

In fact, Alison Van Hoek hadn't even recognized her when she'd first approached Dana about the job. But Dana had remembered the former cheerleader and prom queen—as well as her fiancé, Clark Oxley. They'd all gone to the same high school together, but had moved in two completely different worlds. Dana had never been welcome in Alison's world—until now.

"So, any other big-name clients besides Alison Van Hoek and Hannah Richards?" Debbie asked.

"Those two are at the top of my list," she said, not wanting to reveal that they were the *only* names on her list. Her business thrived on word-of-mouth recommendations. Which meant the Van Hoek wedding, only three weeks away, had to be perfect. Otherwise, her career—and her dreams of a better life—would be over.

"Well, I think I have everything I need," Debbie said, tucking the tape recorder into her tote bag.

"Thank you again." Dana walked her to the door. "If there's ever anything I can do for you..."

"As a matter of fact," Debbie said, "you can give

me the exclusive inside story on the Van Hoek wedding. I wouldn't mind a ringside seat, since all the movers and shakers in Seattle will be there.''

"I'll see what I can do," she replied, opening the door.

That's when she saw a cowboy standing on her doorstep.

He had to be at least six feet three inches, and all of it solid muscle. The man had a roughness about him that went beyond the long, raven-black hair combed straight back off his high forehead. His hair curled ever so slightly at the ends and brushed against broad shoulders that strained the seams of the blue chambray shirt he wore under his faded denim jacket.

Flecks the same shade of blue glimmered in his unusual gray eyes. Eyes that held a hint of danger. Or maybe it was the faded scar on his forehead that sent an apprehensive shiver through her.

He clearly didn't belong here.

"Which one of you is Dana Ulrich?" he asked, his deep voice as smooth as dark whiskey and with more than a hint of a southern accent.

She blinked, surprised that he knew her name. "That would be me."

"I'm here about the wedding of Hannah Richards and Jack McKay."

"And you are…?" Debbie North asked, her brown eyes bright with curiosity.

"Austin Hawke. Brother of the groom."

Dana saw the resemblance now. Hannah Richards had given her an engagement picture of Jack and her to be placed in the society section of the newspaper. Both men were tall and dark, but at least Jack McKay looked civilized. Austin Hawke looked as if he'd stepped out of the Wild West and into a world that was completely foreign to him.

"Please come in," Dana said abruptly, realizing too late that she'd been staring at him. She motioned to the woman beside her. "This is Debbie North, a reporter for the *Seattle Post-Intelligencer*."

Austin tipped his cowboy hat. "It's a pleasure to meet you, ma'am."

"The pleasure is all mine, Mr. Hawke," Debbie said, blushing a little before moving into reporter mode. "Your last name is Hawke, but you're Jack McKay's brother?"

"He's my half brother," Austin clarified.

"Do you live here in Seattle?"

"No, I'm from Texas."

Debbie smiled. "So, you are a *real* cowboy?"

He nodded. "Yes, ma'am."

Anyone could tell that just by looking at his sun-bronzed hands, Dana thought. Broad and rawboned, they were dappled with small scars, a testament to a life of hard, physical labor.

Debbie glanced at her watch with a frown. "I'd love to hear more, but I'm on a deadline." She moved into the hallway. "I'll keep in touch, Dana."

"Great. Thanks again for everything."

When Dana turned around, she caught Austin Hawke staring at her.

"I hope I'm not interrupting anything," he said, taking off his hat.

"Not at all." She moved farther into the living room, then motioned toward the white leather sofa. "Please, have a seat."

The fact that he was a client's brother still didn't explain what the man was doing here. But something told her she was about to find out.

Austin's gaze moved slowly over the room, noting the exposed copper pipes and ductwork running across the ceiling—design elements that made refurbished warehouse apartments like this some of the most sought-after in downtown Seattle. But she could see by the expression on his face that he wasn't too impressed.

"So, what can I do for you, Mr. Hawke?"

His eyes met hers. "The first thing you can do is call me Austin."

She nodded. "All right, Austin."

"I'm here because Jack and Hannah want me to keep an eye on you until the wedding."

Her headache doubled in intensity. "I don't think I understand."

"Hannah hired you to plan their wedding."

"Yes," she said slowly, wondering why Hannah hadn't said anything to her about this.

"Well, I'm here to run interference for Hannah and Jack," he explained. "Any decisions about the wedding will go through me. I plan to be right by your side as you put their wedding together."

The man might be handsome as sin, but Seattle was her town and weddings were her business. Time to put this cowboy out to pasture. "I'm a professional, Mr. Hawke. The last thing I need is a baby-sitter."

"I can see that," he replied, his gaze raking over her in a way that made heat rush into her cheeks. "Your job is to plan this wedding. My job is to take the pressure off Hannah and make sure the day goes off without a hitch.''

Dana shook her throbbing head. ''This is ridiculous. I am perfectly capable of handling everything on my own. If Hannah Richards has any doubts about that, then she shouldn't have hired me.''

''I never said she had doubts about you, although I can't say the same for myself. Didn't the last two weddings you planned end in disaster?''

''That was not my fault,'' she retorted, sounding a little too defensive. ''The brides changed their minds at the last minute. I'm simply a wedding planner, not a relationship counselor.''

''Considering your track record, maybe you should look into a new career.''

Though he'd spoken without malice, his words stung, mostly because she'd been wondering the same thing herself lately. Had she gotten in over her head? Were her dreams just too far out of reach for a girl from the wrong side of the tracks?

No. Dana couldn't give up yet. Not when she still had a fighting chance of making it come true. And the last thing she needed was some Texas cowboy telling her she was in the wrong business. ''I think you'd better leave now.''

Austin rose. ''All right. As long as you understand that any decisions you make regarding Jack and Hannah's wedding will only be done with my approval.''

She laughed aloud at his audacity. ''And what exactly do you know about weddings?''

''Not a damn thing—yet.'' He reached for his cowboy hat. ''But I'm willing to learn.''

She had to remain calm. Professional. "I'm sorry to disappoint you, but I work alone."

"You either work with me or you won't be working on this wedding."

An ultimatum. Dana rose to her feet, her knees shaky. Anger made her head buzz, and she started to see little spots in front of her eyes. As soon as he left, she was going to splurge and break out a can of chicken noodle soup. But first she had to think of something to say that would finally penetrate his thick skull.

Austin's brow creased as he watched her. "You better sit back down."

"I don't take orders from anyone," she replied, an instant before her knees buckled.

Austin was there before she hit the floor. He swept her up into his arms and held her against his broad chest.

It revived her enough to realize she'd almost fainted. Not that she'd ever admit it to him.

"Put me down," she sputtered, planting her palms against his chest.

He obliged, laying her gently on the sofa. "You weigh less than a newborn calf."

"Is that supposed to be a compliment where you come from?"

He didn't answer, reaching behind him for the plate of gourmet chocolates she'd set out for Debbie North. Picking one up, he held it to her mouth. "Eat this."

She shook her head. "Those are Valrhona chocolates. Over ten dollars a pound. They're for my clients and—"

Austin shoved the chocolate truffle in her mouth.

Ecstasy melted on her tongue, and Dana almost moaned aloud at the delicious sensation of the creamy chocolate on her taste buds.

Austin smiled as he watched her chew. "That's much better."

She swallowed. "What gives you the right to come in here and tell me—"

He shoved another truffle between her lips, but he seemed to understand the gist of her question anyway. "Because I owe it to my brother and Hannah. So, whether you like it or not, I'm going to be right by your side as you plan this wedding. I'm going to make sure everything turns out right for them this time."

"This time?" she echoed.

Austin picked up another chocolate truffle and held it to her mouth, but she kept her lips firmly closed, refusing to give in to temptation.

He smiled at her stubbornness. "I know you want it," he said, gently rubbing the chocolate over her lower lip. "I can see it in your eyes."

A strange tingling sensation spread from her lips to other parts of her body. Dana was smart enough not to open her mouth, but that meant she had to sit there as he caressed her lips with that chocolate.

Austin leaned closer to her, his movements almost sensuous, his gray gaze fixed on her mouth. She suddenly found it a little hard to breathe, but blamed that, too, on lack of food.

"You're as stubborn as an old mule," he muttered, finally pulling away and setting the truffle back on the plate.

"So far you've compared me to an old mule and a newborn calf," she said wryly. "I bet you have women falling into haystacks over you back in Texas. Or more likely, jumping off the top of the nearest barn.''

He flashed a grin. ''It sounds like you're starting to feel better.''

She wasn't about to admit he was right, so she didn't say anything.

''When was the last time you ate?''

''Like I said before, I don't need a baby-sitter. I'm perfectly capable of taking care of myself *and* putting together this wedding.''

''Guess you'll have to prove it to me.''

She didn't have to prove anything to him. Dana sat up on the sofa and smoothed back her short hair. ''Let's get this settled once and for all. Are you determined to help me with this wedding?''

''Absolutely.''

''Fine.'' She swung her legs over the couch. ''Then, I'll agree to it as long as we're both perfectly clear that I'm in charge. We go where I want, when I want.''

''You're the expert here, not me.''

''Good.'' She stood up, her knees still a little shaky—a reaction she couldn't entirely blame on low blood sugar. Austin Hawke had a way about him that she found unsettling. Worse, he'd seen her vulnerable. She didn't like to show weakness in front of anyone. Dana had learned a long time ago how dangerous that could be. ''Then, meet me here bright and early tomorrow morning. We have a ten o'clock appointment.''

''Where?'' he asked.

''You'll find out tomorrow. *If* you decide to show up.''

"I'll be here."

She walked unsteadily to the door and pulled it open for him. "Don't be late."

Austin watched her, concern etching his brow. "Are you sure you're all right?"

"Perfect," she said in a clipped tone.

He hesitated a moment, then tipped his hat to her before walking out.

Dana closed the door behind him, resisting the urge to slam it. But she didn't need to resort to such shrewish behavior to get rid of Austin Hawke. She had a knack for reading people. In her occupation, it was a necessity. One look at Austin told her he was a steak-and-a-brew kind of cowboy. A man's man who wouldn't take orders well, especially from a woman.

She could hardly wait for tomorrow to come.

CHAPTER THREE

EARLY THE NEXT MORNING, Austin stood outside Dana's apartment door, his arms too full to knock. So he stuck out one foot and rapped against the solid oak with the toe of his cowboy boot.

He could hear harried footsteps, then a low groan sounded on the other side of the door. Austin bit back a smile, certain she was peering at him through the peephole. Considering her reaction yesterday, he had doubts that she'd let him in.

At last the door opened, just as far as the heavy steel chain lock would allow. Dana scowled out at him through the narrow crack. "What are you doing here?"

"You told me to meet you here in the morning."

"It's not even eight o'clock yet!"

He shrugged, then shifted the grocery bags in his arms. "I usually get up with the sunrise, and that was almost two hours ago."

In truth, he'd wanted to give Jack, Hannah and Adam some time alone together. They'd welcomed him into their home, but he could see the three of them were still adjusting to becoming a family. They didn't need him intruding on their space. So Austin had decided he needed to play invisible as much as possible.

"For your information," Dana said, "most civilized

people do not get up with the sun. You need to expand your cultural horizons, Austin. Many city people don't even go to bed until the sun comes up.''

''Is that why you're not dressed yet?''

She glanced down, as if suddenly aware that she wore nothing more than a pair of pink baby-doll pajamas. Austin had been acutely aware of that fact since the moment she'd opened the door. He'd thought Dana attractive when he first saw her yesterday, with her short black hair and sparkling gray eyes. But now, with her hair tousled and a flush of embarrassment on her cheeks, she was damn pretty.

For a city girl.

Not that Austin had any intention of mixing business with pleasure. He knew her type too well. Fancy apartment. Designer clothes. Even designer chocolate. Dana Ulrich probably wasn't much different from the spoiled Dallas princesses who showed up in country honky-tonks looking for a rough-and-ready cowboy to show them a good time. Austin had been happy to volunteer when he was younger, but he'd soon discovered there wasn't much substance beneath those million-dollar smiles.

Not that Dana was smiling at him now. Her attitude made it clear that she didn't believe he belonged in her high-class world. *Tough.* He was here to stay— temporarily—so she'd better get used to the idea.

Dana moved back behind the door, shielding her body from him. ''Why don't you go away and come back in one hour? Two hours would be even better.''

''Why don't you let me come in and rustle us up some breakfast while you get ready to go?'' Austin countered. "I've got all the fixin's here for a great Tex-Mex omelette."

"Fixin's?" she echoed, her gaze going to the bag in his arm. "Is that cowboy talk for food?"

"Yes, ma'am," he said, exaggerating his Texas drawl.

She shook her head. "You don't have to cook me breakfast."

"Consider it as expanding your cultural horizons," he replied. "Besides, I haven't eaten yet, and you can't expect a man to put in a full day's work on an empty stomach."

He could see the battle in her gorgeous eyes. She didn't want to let him in, but the promise of a hot breakfast tempted her. Which just proved his instincts right yesterday. The woman wasn't eating enough. He'd known that the moment he'd held her in his arms.

She was probably on some crazy fad diet, like eating nothing more than three grapefruits a day. The kind of diet that left so many women looking too bony for his taste. Austin preferred luscious curves he could sink his hands into. Not that he had any intention of sinking his hands into Dana. But he was determined to keep her completely healthy until Jack and Hannah's wedding.

"All right." She relented at last, opening the door wider. "But let's not make this a habit."

"Just point me to the kitchen," Austin said, trying not to stare at her long legs. He looked at her face instead and saw that, even without makeup, her skin was as smooth as fresh cream and her lips the color of wild chokecherries.

"It's that way." She pointed to a swinging door off the living room.

The movement shifted the bodice of her pajama top, giving him a tantalizing glimpse of the curve of her breast. Austin turned away, telling himself to remember why he was here.

"Breakfast," he said aloud, then marched toward the kitchen. "Coming right up."

Dana watched him disappear through the kitchen door, then fled down the hallway to her bedroom. She should have kicked him right out of the apartment! How dare he show up one hour early and then criticize her for the fact that she'd just gotten out of bed.

She couldn't remember the last time a man had made her this angry. Or the last time a man had made her breakfast. But that wasn't the point. Austin Hawke had barged into her life yesterday and attempted to take control.

She couldn't let that happen.

Even if he was tall and rugged and sexy—all the stuff that fantasies were made of. He was also bossy and domineering and a John Wayne wanna-be. Actually, he was more rough around the edges than John Wayne. More talkative than Gary Cooper. Sexier than a young Clint Eastwood.

Definitely a fantasy man.

"Don't go there," Dana admonished herself as she sorted through her closet for something to wear. A man like Austin Hawke might bring out the animal lust in a woman, but he definitely wasn't boyfriend material. Especially for a woman like her, who wanted to move in the right circles. She'd worked too hard to rise above her trailer-park past to backslide now. A cowboy simply didn't fit into her life.

At last she pulled a light blue Liz Claiborne dress out of her closet. She'd found it on sale at a local thrift store. It had a small grease stain on the front, just below the left shoulder pad, but Dana had the perfect pin to hide the spot. Moving to her dresser, she opened the jewelry box on top and pulled out the vintage wreath-shaped pin. It was set with pastel rhinestones and had belonged to her beloved Gram.

As she pinned it to the bodice, Dana vaguely wondered what Gram would have thought of her current predicament. She'd always encouraged Dana to follow her dreams, but the price was getting higher all the time.

If she'd had a choice, Dana would have turned down the Van Hoek wedding. Not because of Alison, but because of the groom, her old high school nemesis Clark Oxley. He was one groom she had no desire to see until the wedding day, and even then, she intended to keep her distance.

Still, Gram would encourage her to fight for what she wanted. And she wanted her career to succeed—with no help from the cowboy currently occupying her kitchen.

Of course, her grandmother had always had a soft spot in her heart for the cowboy hero in the old westerns they used to watch together on television. No doubt she'd have fallen for Austin Hawke's homespun charm.

Good thing Dana was immune to it.

She walked to the bathroom, the seductive aroma of sizzling onions and peppers drifting down the hallway.

She took her time applying her makeup and fixing her hair, even as her mouth began to water. Guilt sneaked up on her when she thought about what she had in store for Austin today. Here he was, fixing her breakfast, while she'd planned a way to get rid of him.

But *why* was he fixing her breakfast? Dana still didn't understand his motive, though a telephone call to Hannah last night had confirmed that Austin had been telling her the truth. Jack and Hannah wanted him to help her plan their wedding.

It still didn't make any sense to her, but Dana was used to brides acting a little irrationally. She just wasn't used to cowboys. Hopefully, she'd found a way to handle this one.

Squaring her shoulders, she walked down the hallway and pushed open the kitchen door.

"Just in time," Austin announced, pulling out a chair for her. He'd hung his cowboy hat on the hook by the door and rolled up his sleeves, revealing dark hair on well-muscled forearms.

Dana sat down at the table, looking in wonder at the bounty in front of her. As well as the omelette on her plate, there were sausages and bacon and fresh-baked biscuits, and a cup of hot cocoa topped with whipped cream.

Austin seated himself across from her. "Hope you're hungry."

"I couldn't eat this much food in a week!"

He picked up his fork. "Don't worry, I can handle the leftovers."

Dana watched him spoon salsa over his omelette, amazed that he could consume that much food in one sitting.

Then he handed the salsa to her. "Here you go."

When had she last eaten an omelette. Or bacon and sausage? Food too expensive for her meager grocery budget.

"I can't believe you actually made all of this. I thought cowboys only ate beans out on the range."

He smiled as he picked up a strip of crisp bacon. "Sounds like you've been watching too many old westerns on television."

That wasn't true, since she'd had the cable disconnected, not able to afford the monthly bill. She might live in Marco's apartment, but she definitely couldn't keep up with his lifestyle. But once her business got off the ground, everything would change. Dana just had to make sure nothing got in her way.

She spooned salsa over her omelette. "So, how did you learn to cook like this? Did your mother teach you?"

His smile faded as he reached for a glass of orange juice. "Actually, I learned to cook after my mom was killed in a car accident. Somebody had to do it. My brother was too busy working cattle and my father was too drunk, so that left me."

"I'm sorry," Dana said hastily, surprised he'd reveal that much to her. Then again, Austin Hawke didn't strike her as a man who kept many secrets. He said exactly what he thought, regardless of the consequences. She had to admit that was a refreshing change from some of the men she'd dated. Irritating, but refreshing.

"Tatiana tells me this isn't your apartment."

She blinked. "Who's Tatiana?"

Austin looked up in surprise. "The Russian redhead

who lives three doors down the hall from you. Haven't you met her?''

"No," she replied, reaching for a biscuit. "I may have seen her in the elevator a few times."

He stared at her. "You rode an elevator with her but you've never talked to her? How is that possible?"

"Because people in this building value their privacy," Dana informed him. "We don't spy on each other or ask nosy questions on the elevator."

"How many people live in this building?"

She shrugged. "About a hundred."

He shook his head in wonderment. "So you live in the same apartment building with these people, but you're all strangers to each other?"

"For the most part." She didn't like the way he made it sound. Cold. Impersonal. "I don't actually live here," she clarified. "I'm just apartment-sitting for a friend who moved to Europe. His lease is up next month, then I'll have to find another place."

"That's what Tatiana told me."

For some reason the thought of the leggy redheaded Russian cozying up to Austin on the elevator annoyed her. "So, what else did she tell you?"

"We talked about a lot of things."

"In a thirty-second elevator ride?"

Austin laid his napkin on his empty plate, then pushed it away. "Actually, she invited me into her apartment for a cup of coffee. She's a flight attendant and had just gotten off work."

Dana gritted her teeth as she stood up and carried her plate to the sink. "You mean you got here even earlier than when you showed up at my door?"

"Around seven," he admitted, before draining the last of his orange juice.

Amazing. She'd lived here two months and didn't know anyone in this building. Austin had been in Seattle one day and had already made friends with the stewardess next door.

He joined her at the sink. "Well, that should hold us over until lunch."

She groaned. "Lunch? Forget it. I'm stuffed. I won't need to eat again until tomorrow."

"Not on my watch," Austin countered. "You're too skinny, Dana, and I'm here to make sure you eat at least three square meals a day."

"Too skinny?" Maybe his honesty wasn't so great, after all. "Haven't you heard that thin is in? Just look at all the cover models and movie stars."

He shook his head. "I don't get the attraction. It would be like making love to a fence post."

"I hope you're not speaking from experience," she said, placing the dishes in the sink.

He laughed. "I'm not attracted to fence posts or bony women. I prefer a woman with definite curves in just the right places."

"Like Tatiana?" Dana blurted out before she could stop herself. The last thing she wanted to talk about was Austin's sex life.

"Tatiana's engaged," Austin replied, "so she's off-limits."

"Most men I know wouldn't let a little thing like an engagement ring stop them," she said, remembering the reason her last bride had bolted. "In fact, they'd think of it as a challenge."

He rinsed out his juice glass. "Then, I guess I'm not like most men."

That was an understatement.

She inhaled the spicy scent of his aftershave and found herself examining his face as he began rinsing the rest of the dishes. The long, lean jaw. The square chin. The unusually thick, dark eyelashes. His eyes were so unusual, misty pools of gray with specks of blue dancing through them.

"What happened there?" she asked, reaching up to brush one soapy fingertip lightly over the faded scar above his eyebrow. She'd noticed it yesterday.

Austin froze for a moment, as if her touch had startled him. Then he cleared his throat and placed a plate in the dish drain. "I sliced it on a barbed-wire fence. Nothing too serious."

"It came awfully close to your eye," she observed. "Sounds like cowboy work can be a little dangerous."

"Sometimes." He met her gaze and a strange heat washed over her.

"How about the job of a wedding planner? Any hidden dangers I should know about?"

The way her heart was pounding, Dana thought the only danger in her life was the man in front of her. He seemed to have a real talent for throwing her off balance. A glance at the clock told her it was time to leave for their ten o'clock appointment.

"You're about to find out," she said, heading toward the door.

AUSTIN DIDN'T KNOW how much more of this he could take. He clenched his jaw, telling himself it would be over soon. All he had to do was hang on a little longer.

"You have to coddle your cuticles," said the man across from him. The man currently holding his hand. "Apply this oil to the base of your fingernails right before you go to bed at night."

Austin gave a brisk nod. He'd learned the hard way that arguing with Paolo about anything tended to make him hysterical. Dana had wanted to check out the Supreme Nail Salon as a possibility for Hannah and Jack, so she'd signed Austin and herself up for a couples manicure. Austin had never had a manicure in his life, and now he knew why.

The temperamental Paolo had filed and buffed and nagged him for the past hour. "Vitamin B tablets are wonderful collagen builders, too." He put down his file and sat back to admire his work. "Perfect, if I do say so myself. Now all we have to do is apply the finishing touch."

Austin swallowed a groan. "We're not done?"

"Almost." Paolo pulled a small bottle out of a drawer. "We just need to apply a little polish and you'll be ready for any occasion."

It was time to draw the line. "I don't wear fingernail polish," Austin stated firmly.

Paolo's brow crinkled. "But it's just a clear lacquer for a nice top coat."

"No polish."

The other man's mouth thinned. "First, you don't want me to file your fingernails. Then you balk at the buffer. You absolutely refuse to even consider acrylics. A nail artist can only take so much."

"You've done a great job," Austin said, trying to placate him. "But where I come from, a man doesn't wear fingernail polish—for any reason."

"But without polish, your nails will be incomplete," Paolo countered. "Like Fred Astaire without Ginger Rogers. Gene Kelly without the umbrella."

"I'm not really much of a dancer."

Paolo scowled at him. "The point is that your hands will be exposed to the harsh, unforgiving elements of sun, wind and rain. I simply can't let that happen."

"Dana," Austin called out, as Paolo began to unscrew the lid on the clear polish.

She looked at him from her manicure table and waved.

He turned back to Paolo, realizing he was on his own. "I'll pay you extra to leave the polish off."

Paolo hesitated, the brush hovering over the bottle. "How much extra?"

Austin shrugged. "How much do you usually charge for a manicure?"

"Thirty dollars is my introductory rate."

Austin's jaw dropped. *"Thirty bucks?"*

"I am an artist," Paolo informed him, drawing up his thin shoulders, "even if *some* people don't appreciate my work." He leaned forward. "Now, if you'd just let me touch up your nails with a little clear polish, you'd see what a difference it can make in your life. Everyone you know will look at you in a new light."

"That's what I'm afraid of," Austin muttered as he reached for his wallet. He tossed two twenty-dollar bills on the table in front of Paolo. "There. That settles it. No polish, no problem. Right?"

Paolo sighed as he scooped up the money. "It's your loss, my friend."

Austin walked over to Dana, ready to get out of this

place before he passed out from the noxious fumes. "Are you almost done?"

"Just finished," she said, rising. She held out her freshly polished pink nails for him to admire. "What do you think?"

"Not bad for thirty bucks."

She looked up at him in surprise. "Thirty bucks? These manicures are complimentary, Austin. It's a common practice in my business, when a salon wants you to recommend them to your clients."

He glanced back at the grinning Paolo. "Now you tell me."

She followed his gaze. "Did you pay him?"

"Yes, but don't worry about it. I'm not about to go ask for my money back."

She smiled up at him. "So you'd recommend this place to your brother?"

"Absolutely not," Austin said, heading toward the door. "Jack wouldn't be caught dead in this place—although it does have the odor of embalming fluid."

"You didn't like your manicure?"

"No," Austin said bluntly. "I'm not a manicure kind of guy. And I can absolutely guarantee you that Jack wouldn't like one, either."

"That's too bad," Dana replied. "I've already made arrangements for Hannah and her bridesmaids to come in for full manicures the day before the wedding. I thought I'd do the same for Jack and his groomsmen."

"Only if you want a matrimonial mutiny on your hands," Austin muttered.

"Paolo thought it was a good idea," Dana argued. "He's trying to increase his male clientele."

Austin turned to her. "Just so we're completely

clear—that is the first and last time I will ever let Paolo or any other man hold my hand. The manicure is out.''

"Okay," she said with a smile that made him a little suspicious. "If you're sure."

"I'm sure," he said. "Now, what's next?"

"The pedicure."

He stared at her. "What did you say?"

Paolo approached him with a towel slung over his shoulder. "Your footbath awaits."

Anger coming to a slow boil, Austin turned to Dana. He'd had enough of this silly game. "It won't work."

"What won't work?" she asked innocently.

"Trying to scare me off."

Paolo looked back and forth between them. "Is there a problem?"

"Not at all," Dana assured him. "Just give us a few moments alone."

"Very well."

Austin waited until the manicurist was out of earshot before he said, "I'm not backing off, Dana. No matter how many Paolos you throw in my path."

"Pedicures can be quite relaxing. Or perhaps you'd prefer a facial?"

His gaze narrowed. "You're playing with fire, city girl."

"We agreed last night that I'm in charge." She peered over his shoulder. "Paolo's headed this way again. I need to maintain a good relationship with my vendors."

"We're leaving."

She planted her hands on her hips. "We're staying."

The woman didn't leave him any choice. He bent

down and hoisted her over his shoulder, carrying her out the door of the salon. Several of the patrons gasped at the sight.

For a moment, Dana didn't move, obviously too shocked by his take-charge attitude. Then she began to beat at his back with her fists.

"Put me down!"

So he did—sliding her off his shoulder and down his body, until her feet were firmly on the ground. The physical contact made his anger turn into something else entirely.

Her cheeks flushed a bright pink and quicksilver flashed in her eyes. "What do you think you're doing? Maybe things are different in Texas, but this *is* the twentieth century, not the Stone Age!"

Damn, she was pretty. "All those fumes must have affected my thinking."

"This is not funny. You've just humiliated me in front of everyone in that salon!"

"I'm sorry," he said, and meant it.

"*Sorry* is not enough," she cried. "Not nearly enough. This is— This is…" Dana seemed to be at a loss for words, too outraged by the way he had manhandled her to even think straight.

Austin had the same problem. Because even though he knew he'd been wrong, all he could think about at that moment was how much he wanted to taste that sassy mouth of hers. He took a step closer to her, his entire body thrumming with anticipation.

She looked up into his eyes, finally finding the perfect words to describe the situation between them. "This is crazy."

"I know."

Then he kissed her.

CHAPTER FOUR

DANA SAW IT COMING, but she couldn't move. Desire flashed in his eyes, then his mouth was hard on hers. His lips branded her with a white-hot intensity that melted into her bones, and she had to reach out and grab his shoulders just to keep her balance.

It was over all too soon. Austin jerked away from her, muttering a curse under his breath.

She gasped for air, as shocked by her reaction as by the kiss itself.

"Hell," he said, breathing deeply.

Dana thought just the opposite. That kiss had been pure heaven. Maybe those salon fumes were affecting her thinking as well as his. She took a deep, steadying breath.

"What just happened here?"

"I guess I got caught up in the heat of the moment," Austin said, stepping away from her.

Heat was definitely the right word for it. It still crackled in her veins and dissolved the righteous indignation she'd felt only a few moments earlier.

This *was* crazy. Insane. She could *not* be attracted to a cowboy from Texas.

"Are you all right?" he asked, apparently unnerved by her silence.

Good question. The chirp of her cellular phone gave

her a welcome reprieve. She fished the phone out of her purse and flipped it open.

"Hello?"

"Good morning, Dana, this is Alison."

"Hi, Alison. What can I do for you?"

"Well, I have some good news and some bad news."

"What's the bad news?" She could feel Austin's steady gaze on her and for some reason it made her self-conscious. Smoothing down her hair with her free hand, she tried to regain her composure.

"My future mother-in-law came up with fifty more people she wants to invite to the reception."

Alison Van Hoek had insisted on a small, old-fashioned wedding at Our Lady of Mercy Catholic church. Unfortunately, the mother of the groom didn't seem to understand the meaning of the word *small*. They'd finally compromised by giving Mrs. Oxley free rein to invite anyone she wished to the reception to be held in the grand ballroom of the Palace Hotel. But at this rate, even that wouldn't hold all the guests.

"But, Alison, I already sent all the invitations out last week."

"I know it's a pain," Alison said with groan, "but can't we find some way to squeeze just a few more people in?"

Fifty people were more than a few. Alison was bright and bubbly, just as she'd been in high school, but she was definitely making Dana earn her fee for this wedding. At the very least, it would mean making changes to the caterer's menu, adjusting the seating arrangement at the reception, and allowing for additional tables, chairs and centerpieces. All in less than three weeks.

"Sure," Dana said at last. "I'll find a way to make room for them."

"Wonderful!"

"As soon as you give me the new list, I'll send out the additional invitations."

"I'll fax it to you this afternoon," Alison promised. "Now for my good news."

"I can't wait to hear it."

"Clark wants to be more involved in the wedding."

Dana tensed. "What exactly does that mean?"

"Well, my fiancé's been feeling a little neglected. He thinks I care more about the wedding than I do about him. So I suggested he pitch in to help us, and he agreed!"

"It's not uncommon for the groom to feel sidelined when planning a wedding," Dana said, not wanting to come within a hundred feet of Clark Oxley until absolutely necessary. "Maybe if you tell him those feelings are perfectly normal...."

"No way," Alison said. "If he's willing to help, I'm not going to argue with him. I think it's sweet."

"The wedding is only three weeks away," Dana told her. "Most of the details have already been worked out."

"I know, but there are still a few decisions to be made. Clark gets back from a business trip on Friday, so I thought I'd bring him over to your place that evening, if you're free, so you can fill him in on all the details."

Friday was only three days away. Dana wished it

were more like three thousand. "I'll have to check my calendar."

Something in her tone must have caught Austin's attention. He moved a step closer, concern etched on his brow.

"Let me know," Alison said. "Oh, and I haven't told him that you went to high school with us at Westwood. I can't wait to see if he remembers you. Just pretend you've never met him before."

If only that were true.

"I'll do my best," Dana replied. She was tempted to make up an excuse for Friday night, even though she knew her schedule was free. But why delay the inevitable? "Actually, now that I think about it, that day should work just fine."

"Great!" Alison exclaimed. "I'm not sure what time we'll get there. It depends when Clark's flight comes in."

Dana tried to sound upbeat. "Anytime will be fine."

"Okay, we'll see you then."

"Bye." Dana switched off the phone, then dropped it back in her purse.

She looked up at Austin. That phone call had erased all the warm, fuzzy feelings his kiss had generated. The reality was that she didn't have time to play games with him. Or with herself.

"I need to make one thing perfectly clear," she said firmly. "If we're going to work together, what just happened between us can't happen again."

"It was a mistake," he admitted, a muscle flexing in his jaw. "A big mistake."

For some reason, that admission made her feel

worse. "All right." She turned toward her car. "Let's just pretend it never happened."

"If that's the way you want it," he replied, following her into the parking lot.

"It is." She'd driven them to the nail salon this morning, though her fifteen-year-old car was less than reliable. A fact it proved once again when it wouldn't start for her.

"Come on," Dana prodded, pumping the gas pedal. *Can anything else go wrong today?*

"Want me to try it?" Austin offered.

"It takes a certain touch," she replied, rewarded for her patience when the engine finally roared to life. She patted the dashboard. "Good job."

"You talk to your car?"

"The Beast behaves better when I talk to it."

A smile tipped up one corner of his mouth. "The Beast?"

"That's what my Gram called it," Dana explained. "She left me the car in her will. She didn't learn to drive until my grandpa died, so this was the first and only car she ever owned. She loved it."

"And now it belongs to you," Austin said. "Beauty and the Beast."

Dana gave him a sidelong glance, not sure if he was teasing her or flirting with her. She decided it was the former, since he'd just confessed that kissing her was a big mistake.

He turned on the radio. "Do you have any country music stations in Seattle?"

"I wouldn't know," she replied, turning onto the street.

"Here we go," he said with a smile, tuning in a station. "I love the Dixie Chicks."

She'd never heard of them, but found herself enjoying the upbeat music. Then she turned to Austin. "Am I wrong or are they singing about poisoning some guy with black-eyed peas?"

"That's what the song's about," he affirmed. "It's called 'Goodbye, Earl.'"

"Interesting," Dana mused.

Austin settled back in his seat. "So, how about lunch? My treat."

"Sorry, but I don't have time. I have to meet with the priest of the Van Hoek wedding at one o'clock."

"Van Hoek?"

"Alison Van Hoek," she clarified. "Her wedding is in three weeks. It's going to be huge—the reception, anyway. Four hundred people." Then she remembered Alison's bad news. "Make that four hundred and fifty."

He shook his head. "What a nightmare."

She glanced over at him. "Why do you say that?"

"Weddings should be for close friends and family. Not some kind of spectacle."

"The ceremony itself will be relatively small," Dana explained. "The church only holds about two hundred people."

"You call that a small wedding?"

"Relatively speaking." Dana turned down the volume on the radio. "It's going to be beautiful. Floral sprays decorating the end of each pew. Six attendants for the bride and groom. A bridal gown with imported lace, designed by Marco Kahn himself. A hundred trained white doves released as the bride and groom leave the church. The ceremony will be followed by a sit-down dinner reception at the Palace Hotel, which is owned by the groom's family.''

"And how much is this extravaganza going to cost?''

She gave a slight shrug, mentally calculating in her head. "I'd say about mid five figures.''

He stared at her. "Fifty thousand dollars for trained doves and imported lace?''

She tipped up her chin. "There's a lot more to it than that.''

"I could buy a quarter section of good pasture ground for fifty thousand dollars,'' Austin said in amazement. "Or a herd of Angus breeding heifers. I can't believe people actually waste that much money for something that only lasts one day.''

Dana bristled at his easy dismissal of her life's work. "The wedding itself might only last a day, but the memories will last a lifetime.''

"Or until the divorce.''

She arched a brow. "So you don't believe in happily every after?''

"It's great for fairy tales, but I've heard the statistics. One out of every two marriages doesn't last. Seems like a lot of money to put on the line, with those kind of odds.''

"I think of it as an investment in the future,'' Dana countered. "A good foundation to build a marriage on.''

"A marriage should be built on love and trust,'' Austin argued. "If you don't have those two things, it doesn't matter how much money you throw at it.''

She pulled to the curb in front of her apartment building, parking right behind his truck. "I think we're just going to have to agree to disagree on this point.''

"All right," Austin said, reaching for the door handle. "But no trained doves for Jack and Hannah's wedding."

"You don't know what you're missing."

His molten gray eyes met hers. "I think I do."

Something told her that he wasn't talking about trained doves anymore.

She looked straight ahead. "We have an appointment tomorrow afternoon at the European Bakery to pick out Jack and Hannah's wedding cake. Unless… Do you want me to handle the rest of the wedding plans on my own?"

His gaze narrowed on her. "Like I said before, I'm not backing off."

Dana's plan to scare him away had backfired. Maybe it was time to just accept the inevitable. "The bakery is on Delancey Street. Meet me there at two o'clock."

"I'll be there," he promised, then climbed out of her car.

She pulled away from the curb and turned in to the parking garage. Funny how her conversation with Austin had temporarily put Clark Oxley's impending visit completely out of her mind.

But now dread settled low in her stomach. Would Clark look the same as he had ten years ago? Or worse, act the same? Then she tried to see the bright side. Alison had matured from a ditzy, self-absorbed cheerleader into someone who treated her with respect. Maybe Clark had changed as well.

If not, she was in big trouble.

THE NEXT THREE DAYS were sheer torture for Dana. Not only did she worry about her upcoming reunion with Clark Oxley, but Austin seemed determined to oppose her at every turn.

Or maybe he was just trying to drive her crazy.

Like suggesting the chocolate groom's cake for Hannah and Jack's wedding be shaped like the state of Texas. Or asking the photographer if he charged by the hour or by the picture. Or insisting that she consider serving an old-fashioned Texas barbecue for the catered reception.

By Friday evening, her nerves were completely frazzled.

Waiting alone in her apartment for Alison and Clark to arrive, she fluffed the pillows on the sofa at least three times, then picked up tiny bits of lint from the floor.

She'd artfully arranged the few remaining Valrhona chocolates into a star pattern and set them on a vintage china plate on the coffee table. Then she took a slow turn around the room, making sure everything was perfect.

A muted knock sounded at the door, and her heart skipped a beat.

"Relax," she chided herself, walking to the door. She wanted Clark to see her as cool and calm. The ultimate professional. She pasted a smile on her face, then opened the door.

"Howdy." Austin stood on the threshold, a sack in each arm.

"What are you doing here?" she cried.

"I came to convince you that Texas barbecue is the way to go," he replied, walking inside. "Hope you're hungry."

"We are not serving Texas barbecue at the reception," she said firmly. "For one thing, it's an early-afternoon wedding, so a buffet of hors d'oeuvres is more appropriate than a full meal. Something light but satisfying, like Oriental food. I think appetizers such as dim sum and miniature egg rolls would go over very well and give a nice exotic touch."

"Darlin'," he drawled, "if you want exotic, try some Lonestar specialties like barbecued rattlesnake or prairie oysters."

"Prairie oysters?"

"A real delicacy." He grinned. "I've never been partial to them myself, but some folks get a real craving when it's time to castrate the bull calves."

"Castrate?" She paled. "You mean they eat the…"

He nodded. "Deep-fried."

She grimaced. "There goes my appetite."

"Look, I'm not suggesting we serve rattlesnake or prairie oysters at the wedding reception. But can't we at least add some Tex-Mex flavor to the menu?"

Before she could reply, the doorbell rang.

He arched a brow. "Expecting company?"

She nodded, her mouth suddenly dry. "Alison Van Hoek and her fiancé. I'm going to have to ask you to leave."

"No problem," he said, heading for the door.

A vision of him meeting Clark and talking about prairie oysters flashed in her mind. "Why don't you go out this way," she suggested, heading him off and turning him toward the swinging door. "There's another door off the kitchen that leads to the service elevator. It's much faster. I always take it when I'm in a hurry.''

"Is there a reason you're trying to sneak me out the back door?'' he asked, arching a dark brow. ''Are you afraid I'll embarrass you in front of your fancy friends?''

''They're not my friends,'' she clarified. *Far from it.* Just the thought of Clark Oxley sneering at Austin's cowboy hat and country manners made her cringe inside. ''They're very important clients and I'd rather not have to explain what you're doing here.''

''I came here to fix you dinner,'' he stated as the doorbell rang again. ''That doesn't seem like a complicated explanation to me.''

She didn't have time to argue.

''Please, Austin, just go.''

He hesitated a moment, then spun around and pushed open the kitchen door. As it swung shut behind him, she turned and ran to the front, pausing just long enough to take a deep, calming breath.

Then she opened the door.

Clark Oxley looked almost exactly as he had ten years ago. Thick blond hair that curled slightly at his neck. Sky-blue eyes that twinkled when he smiled. A deep cleft in his chin.

He was one of those people that didn't age. A man who would look as good at fifty-eight as he did at twenty-eight.

''Hi, Dana,'' Alison said, as they walked into the apartment. A mischievous gleam shone in her green eyes when she made the introductions. ''This is my fiancé, Clark Oxley. Clark, this is our wedding planner, Dana Ulrich.''

Her entire body tensed as Clark's gaze met her own. But there was no flicker of recognition on his face. Only a polite smile as he held out his hand.

"Nice to meet you, Dana," he said. "Alison tells me you have everything under control."

"That's my job," she said, having no choice but to shake his hand. His skin was cool, his grip firm. She slipped her hand out of his, resisting the urge to wipe it on her slacks.

"This is a great place," Clark said, glancing around. "I've been looking for a downtown apartment for Alison and me to move into after we're married."

"I like it," Dana replied, not telling him that it would soon be up for rent again. Clark might be a client, but she didn't owe him anything except a professionally planned wedding.

"Clark's been living in a suite at the Palace Hotel," Alison explained. "Personally, I love the idea of round-the-clock room service, but he wants us to find a place of our own after the honeymoon."

"Please come in and sit down," Dana said when she realized they were all still standing in the foyer. "Here, let me take your coats."

Alison pulled her wool jacket more tightly around her as she walked into the living room. "I think I'll keep mine on for a while. I'm a little cold."

"Why don't I make some coffee?" Dana suggested, taking Clark's coat and hanging it in the hall closet. "Then we can talk about the wedding."

"That sounds wonderful," Alison replied, seating herself on the sofa.

Dana escaped into the kitchen, giving herself a few moments to relax and regroup. Their meeting hadn't been as traumatic as she'd imagined. Clark had been polite and friendly, completely oblivious to her real feelings about him.

So far, so good.

After plugging in the coffeepot, she reached into the cupboard for the imported gourmet coffee she kept for her clients.

"Can I lend you a hand?"

She whirled to see Clark standing just inside the doorway. "Where's Alison?"

"She's on a cell phone call with her mother." He smiled as he moved farther into the kitchen, letting the door swing closed behind him. "Once those two start talking, it's hard to get them to stop."

Dana told herself to stay calm, but that was hard to do with her heart racing in her chest. "I really don't need any help in here. Thanks, anyway."

"Are you sure?" he asked, moving beside her. "I'm pretty handy in the kitchen."

"I'm positive."

But Clark didn't leave. Instead he moved even closer and said in a low voice, "I remember you, Dana."

She swallowed as she met his gaze, determined not to let him intimidate her. "Do you?"

He nodded. "We all attended Westwood High School together. Class of 1994."

A class she'd tried hard to forget. Those high school years had been so miserable for her. Now two of those classmates held her future in their hands. At this moment, the pain of the past threatened to overwhelm her.

"Does Alison know?" he asked, his gaze intent on her face.

"Yes," Dana replied, "but only because I told her. She didn't remember me."

"That's not what I meant," he said, shaking his head. "Does Alison know about the…misunderstanding you and I had in high school?"

"There was no misunderstanding," she retorted, old emotions bubbling to the surface and making her voice shake. "You tried to bully me into having sex with you, and when I refused, you made my life hell. Harassing me in the hallways. Groping me every chance you got. Destroying my reputation."

"Keep your voice down," he exclaimed, glancing toward the kitchen door. "You're overreacting. Besides, that all happened a long time ago. We were just dumb teenagers. No good can come of dredging it up again now."

If only she could dismiss the past so easily. But it had almost destroyed her, making Dana believe she was worthless. Now she was out to prove to people like Clark, and to herself, that she could succeed. That the girl her upper-crust classmates had called a trailer-trash tramp—and worse—could fit into their world.

Dana took a deep breath, realizing that no matter how much she despised Clark, she couldn't afford to antagonize him. The wedding of Alison Van Hoek and Clark Oxley could make or break her career.

"You're right. It's in the past. Let's keep it there."

He gave a brisk nod, relief shining in his blue eyes. "Good decision."

As he turned around to walk out of the kitchen, Dana released a silent sigh of relief. But the next thing she knew, the pantry door swung open and Austin stepped right into his path.

"Howdy." Austin's friendly tone belied the homicidal sparks in his eyes.

Clark assessed the man in front of him, from Austin's snakeskin cowboy boots all the way to his black cowboy hat. "Hello."

When she saw Austin's hand curl into a fist, Dana stepped forward, placing herself squarely between the two men. "Clark, this is Austin Hawke. Austin, this is Clark Oxley, Alison Van Hoek's fiancé."

Clark stuck out his pale hand. "It's a pleasure to meet you."

Austin clasped Clark's hand in his own, squeezing firmly. "The pleasure's all mine."

Clark's smile quickly faded as Austin applied more pressure to the handshake.

Dana couldn't help the twinge of satisfaction deep inside her at the growing discomfort she saw on Clark's face.

Then the kitchen door opened and Alison walked inside. "Hey, what's everybody doing in here?"

Reaching out, Dana lightly touched Austin's forearm, silently imploring him to drop Clark's hand. He did, then wiped his own hand on the side of his jeans.

Dana could feel the tension crackling between the two men. Tension she had to find a way to diffuse. "I was just introducing Clark to...my boyfriend."

Alison's eyes widened as she looked at Austin. "Really? What a surprise!"

Judging by the expression on Austin's face, he was just as surprised. She gave him a tentative smile, hoping he wouldn't expose her lie. Not when she had so much at stake.

"I had no idea you were even dating anyone," Alison said.

Austin circled his arm around Dana's waist and hauled her close to his side. "She's a little shy."

"Oh, I just love your southern accent!" Alison exclaimed.

Clark didn't say anything. He just stood there and rubbed his sore hand.

"This is Austin Hawke," Dana said, all too aware of the way his hard warm body was pressed against her own. "Austin, this is Alison Van Hoek."

He tipped his hat to her. "Ma'am."

Alison laughed. "You sound just like a real cowboy."

One corner of Austin's mouth hitched up in a smile. "I am a real cowboy, so I'll take that as a compliment."

"Oh, it is," Alison said, then turned to her fiancé. "Now, tell me what you three have been doing in here without me."

"I came to lend Dana a hand," Clark said smoothly, with no trace of his earlier tension. "Did you know she went to our high school?"

"I wondered how long it would take for you to figure that out," Alison admitted, playfully poking him in the ribs. "I didn't recognize Dana at all. And you didn't recognize her either, did you?"

"Not at first," Clark said, draping one arm around his fiancée's shoulders as he met Dana's gaze. "But something about her seemed familiar."

Dana sensed an insult in his words, even though they sounded innocent enough. Was she overreacting? She'd spent her high school years enduring his unrelenting sexual harassment. But as much as she hated to admit it, Clark was right. They weren't teenagers anymore. He hadn't said or done anything offensive to her since walking through her door this evening— other than trivializing the way he'd treated her ten years ago.

For the first time, she realized it probably *had* been trivial for him. While she had agonized over her inability to fit in at Westwood High, Clark had been enjoying all the pleasures and privileges that came with being one of the most popular boys in school.

The last thing she wanted to do was give Clark the satisfaction of believing his past harassment still bothered her. Especially when the truth was that she'd channeled all that frustration and anger and pain into striving for a better life. A life no one could ridicule.

"I even looked up Dana's picture in the yearbook," Alison told him, "but she doesn't look the same at all. We must not have been in any classes together."

They'd been in English and Algebra together, but Dana wasn't surprised that Alison didn't remember her. She'd always tried to be invisible.

"We had four hundred kids in our graduating class," Dana said, "so it's hard to keep track anymore."

"True," Alison replied, smiling up at her fiancé. "Clark and I even lost track of each other after high school—until he hired my design firm to refurbish the Palace Hotel last year. Then it was like we'd never been apart."

"You're an impossible woman to forget," Clark said, kissing her forehead.

Dana glanced up at Austin and saw a muscle flex in

his jaw. His disdain of Clark was almost palpable. He obviously didn't know the Oxleys were one of the most powerful families in Seattle.

"Hey, I've got an idea," Alison said. "Why don't you two come to the Valentine's Day dance at the club with us next weekend. You can be our guests."

"The club?" Austin echoed.

"The Highland Country Club," Clark informed him, then turned to Alison. "I'm not sure Mr. Hawke would be comfortable there. We don't have any horses."

"Very funny," Alison replied with a grin. "I think it will be a blast. A bunch of the old gang will be there from school, including two of my bridesmaids. We could talk about the wedding, and old times."

The last thing Dana wanted to do was dredge up old times, but she'd be a fool to pass up an invitation like that. Highland Country Club was her entrée into the world of the Seattle elite. They liked to spend big money, especially on the weddings of their sons and daughters.

"We'd love to come," Dana said.

"Great." Alison glanced at her watch. "We're supposed to meet my parents in about an hour for a late dinner. Shall we go ahead and get started filling Clark in on all the wedding plans?"

"Of course," Dana said. "You two go on into the living room. Just let me pour us some coffee and I'll join you in a minute."

Alison smiled up at Austin. "It was nice to meet you. I look forward to seeing you next weekend."

"Ma'am," he said, tipping his hat as she followed her fiancé out the kitchen door. When they were gone, he turned to Dana. "Now, do you want to tell me what the hell that was all about?"

"Later," she promised, pouring two cups of steaming coffee. "I'm free tomorrow if you want to stop by—"

Austin wasn't about to let her put him off. "I'll wait right here until your meeting is over."

Dana thought he'd get tired of waiting for her, but she discovered that Austin Hawke was a man of his word when she returned to the kitchen an hour later.

He was sitting at the table, an almost empty pot of her expensive gourmet coffee in front of him. She swallowed the impulse to chastise him for drinking it, realizing she owed him at least that much for going along with her charade earlier.

"Are they gone?" he asked.

She nodded as she deposited a tray of empty coffee cups on the counter. "They just left."

Austin stood up. "The question is why you'd let a man like Clark Oxley into your home in the first place."

Dana turned to face him, her shoulders aching with tension. Even though he'd treated her with nothing but politeness, playing nice with Clark for the last hour had worn on her nerves. Still, his behavior was a welcome change from high school. Maybe he really had grown up.

"Clark is a client," she replied.

Austin folded his arms across his chest. "It sounded to me like he was more than that."

Dana realized she owed him an explanation, since she'd brought him into this mess. She just wasn't sure where to start. "Clark and I have a...history."

A dark eyebrow shot up. "Care to elaborate?"

"I think you already heard most of it while you were hiding in the pantry. Clark didn't like the fact that I rejected his advances in high school, so he made me pay for it."

"You were the one who wanted me to hide from your clients," he reminded her.

"What were you doing in the pantry, anyway?" she asked, welcoming the change of subject. "I thought you'd left."

"I was taking inventory. When I was making breakfast the other morning, I noticed that most of your cupboards, as well as your refrigerator, were practically bare." He frowned. "Exactly what kind of starvation diet are you on?"

The insufficient funds diet, she thought wryly, but didn't say it aloud. "That's not your concern."

"Maybe not." Austin walked up behind her and turned her to face him. "But the fact that you let a jerk like Clark Oxley back into your life after the way he treated you concerns me."

"When Alison approached me to plan her wedding, we didn't get around to discussing the name of her fiancé until after I'd already accepted the job. To tell the truth, I'm not sure if it would have made a difference anyway. This is going to be the biggest society wedding of the season."

He looked at her as if she spoke a foreign language he didn't understand. "So?"

"So...ever since *Seattle Magazine* dubbed me the wedding jinx, my business, the career I've dreamed about since I was sixteen years old, has been on the brink of oblivion! I *need* this job, Austin. It's a matter of survival."

"You've got Hannah and Jack's wedding," he reminded her.

"And I'm grateful for it," she told him. "But the Van Hoek wedding can make my career. It's going to be splashed across the society pages of every newspaper in this city. And I consider the four hundred and fifty guests at the reception as potential future customers. There's no way I could turn it down."

Austin clenched his jaw. "Does Alison know about the way he used to harass you?"

"No," she said, sucking in a deep breath. "At least, I never told her."

"Don't you think she has a right to know?"

She shook her head, fearing he would never understand. "It's old news."

"That's for Alison to decide," he replied. "I think she has a right to know her fiancé used to grope her wedding planner and sexually harass her on a daily basis."

"That was ten years ago. Clark didn't do either one of those things tonight. Maybe he's matured since high school."

"A rattlesnake might shed its skin but it's still a rattlesnake."

Now it was her turn to challenge him. "You don't believe people can change?"

"No," he said bluntly.

She stared at him in amazement, his attitude in direct contrast to her own. Dana had to believe people could change—that *she* could change—or her future would become as grim as her past. "Why not?"

"Because we're not built that way. You can't exchange your personality at the local department store for a new one. Or your values. They're ingrained in us from an early age. They make us who we are."

"I disagree. Humans have been evolving for centuries. We've had to change to survive."

"Believe me, men like Clark don't change. He reminds me of my old man, who had a mean streak a mile deep. Yet he could charm anyone he pleased—when it suited him."

Now she understood some of his animosity. At least her parents had provided a loving haven from the bullies at school. Judging by the stark expression on Austin's face, he hadn't been so fortunate.

"So you believe Clark's just trying to charm me?" she asked at last.

"You and Alison both—for as long as it suits him."

She considered his words. "Even if I did tell her the truth, what makes you think Alison would believe me?"

"Why wouldn't she believe you?"

"My high school counselor didn't," Dana blurted out before she could stop herself.

Austin's indignation faltered. "What?"

She swallowed hard, hating to relive memories she'd pushed so far back in her mind. "This whole problem started when Clark asked me out on a date when we were both in high school. I was thrilled that a guy like him would even notice me. He was one of the most popular boys in our class."

"That's hard to believe."

His comment made her smile. But her smile faded when she remembered how that dream date had turned into a nightmare. "I thought we were going to a movie, but we only got as far as a deserted parking lot. He'd brought me there to make out with him."

Austin stood next to her, his large frame oddly comforting instead of intimidating. "But you turned him down."

She nodded. "He didn't take it well. When I finally convinced him I meant it, he ordered me out of his car and told me he was too good for a trailer-park tramp, anyway."

"Bastard," Austin growled.

"The next day Clark bragged to his football buddies that I was easy. A slut. They all started propositioning me—harassing me. So I went to the school guidance counselor."

"And?"

"And she didn't believe me." Dana relaxed a little now that the worst part of her story was out in the open. Funny how confiding her best-kept secret had actually made her feel better.

"You have to understand," she continued. "Clark Oxley's mother was on the school board. He was on the football team and a member of the National Honor Society. A golden boy. I was trailer-park trash."

His gray gaze burned into her. "You are not trash."

"I know that...now. But nobody believed me back then. So why should I believe that Alison would take my word over that of her fiancé?"

"Just tell her everything you just told me. Or I'll do it for you."

"No." Dana shook her head. "Absolutely not. She'll wonder why neither one of us told her the truth the moment she walked into the kitchen. It's too late.

I'm not going to sacrifice my business and my career because of Clark Oxley. I won't let him win again.''

Austin moved a step closer to her, his jaw tight. ''I think you're letting him win now. What's to stop him from pulling the same kind of crap again?''

''Because I'm not eighteen anymore,'' she said with more confidence than she felt. ''Besides, he won't do or say anything if he thinks I'm dating another man. Especially a man who could break his fingers with a handshake.''

His nostrils flared. ''I'd like to break a lot more than the jerk's fingers.''

She swallowed, aware that she was asking a lot of him. ''Will you do it? Will you play the part of my boyfriend?''

Austin considered her proposition. ''What's in it for me?''

CHAPTER FIVE

HIS QUESTION caught her off guard. Austin didn't strike her as an opportunist. But then, as her story had just demonstrated, she'd been wrong about men before.

"What do you want?"

He didn't pause a beat. "I want to move in here with you."

At first she thought he was joking. But there wasn't a hint of humor in his flinty gray eyes. "For what possible reason?"

"I have two reasons, actually. The first is to protect you from that creep Oxley."

"We don't know for sure that he's still a creep, but even if he is, I'm perfectly capable of protecting myself."

"I disagree on both counts," he said. "But the second reason is that I don't feel comfortable staying at Jack's place anymore. The three of them need time alone together to become a family."

She admired his reasons, just not his solution. "You certainly won't be comfortable here. This apartment only has one bedroom."

"I can bunk on the living room floor," Austin said. "I've slept outside on more cattle drives than I can count, so this will definitely be a step up."

"W-we hardly know each other," Dana stammered, trying to find some hole in his logic. "We just met a few days ago."

"I know you're too stubborn and too skinny for your own good, but for a city girl, you're not bad."

"Gee, thanks," she mused, less than flattered by his description. Not that she was out to impress Austin, especially since they saw the world so differently.

Still, the thought of him moving in with her was oddly unsettling. She couldn't pinpoint the reason, but part of it might have to do with the way he was looking at her right now. His gray gaze was unflinching and much too perceptive. Dana worked hard to maintain a certain image, but Austin had no patience with illusions. He preferred cold, harsh reality.

"It won't work," she said at last.

"Why not?"

She frantically searched her mind for a reason that would dissuade him. "I talk in my sleep. That's sure to keep you awake at night."

One corner of his mouth hitched up in a smile. "Might be entertaining."

"I'm a lousy cook."

"Then, I'll do the cooking."

She emitted a sigh of exasperation. "You have an answer for everything."

"What's the real reason you don't want me here?" he asked. Then his tone gentled. "Are you afraid to be alone with me?"

"No," Dana replied honestly.

He had never done anything to make her fear him. Even when he'd carried her out of the nail salon, she hadn't been scared. Shocked and angry, but not afraid. On the contrary, Austin made her feel safe.

"Maybe it will work," she admitted.

"If you're determined to go through with the Van Hoek wedding, what better way to convince good old Clark that you're off-limits?"

Dana couldn't argue with that. Finding herself alone in the kitchen with Clark *had* unnerved her. What if he returned to her apartment when she was alone? She didn't need a man to protect her, but she couldn't deny that having Austin here would give her peace of mind.

"I'll move in tonight," Austin said, as if it was already decided.

"First we need to set some ground rules." Dana might have conceded to let him move in with her, but she fully intended to maintain control of the situation. "And the first rule is that I make all the rules."

Austin cocked a brow. "Is that so?"

She nodded. "It's my apartment. Well, Marco's apartment, but I'm in charge."

"I've never been too fond of rules."

"The second rule," Dana continued, as if he hadn't spoken, "is that there won't be any more physical contact between us."

He folded his arms across his chest. "Such as?"

Her face warmed. "You know what I mean. That kiss outside the nail salon the other day. And the way you held me in the kitchen this evening."

"I don't seem to recall you objecting either time."

"The kiss caught me completely off guard. And I could hardly complain about my boyfriend putting his arm around me, with Alison and Clark standing right in front of us."

"Any other rules?"

"No country music on the CD player."

He placed a hand over his heart. "Now, that hurts."

"I mean it," Dana replied. "I'm sticking with strictly classical music because a potential client could stop by at any moment and I need to project a certain image. Which brings me to you."

"Me?"

"Your image is all wrong. For Seattle, I mean."

"My image? I'm a cowboy, Dana. Nothing more, nothing less. Life is about how you live, not how you look."

He sounded so sure of himself. She wondered what it would feel like to have that kind of self-confidence. Then again, he spent most of his time with cows.

Dana knew the members of the Highland Country Club wouldn't see beyond his boots and cowboy hat to the man underneath. They'd all make fun of him. Mock him. She couldn't let that happen.

"A simple shopping trip to buy you some new clothes," she persisted. "How bad could that be?"

"I'm not going to waste good money on clothes I'll never wear again."

She decided to let it go for now. "All right, we can talk about it later."

"So it's all settled? I'll move in and start playing your boyfriend?"

She hesitated, still not completely convinced it was a good idea. On the other hand, what did she have to lose? "Why not? I'll have a key made for you."

"And I'll go pack my bags." He turned to leave, then spun back around and put one arm around Dana's waist, pulling her tightly against him.

When she opened her mouth to protest, he kissed her long and deep, staking claim to her in a way that left her breathless. It was over in a moment, leaving Dana too shocked to say a word.

"See what I mean about following rules?" He winked at her, then he was gone.

No man had ever kissed her like Austin did. The other day he'd said kissing her was a mistake. But now he was playing her boyfriend, a role he fell into all too easily. Maybe she did have something to lose, after all.

Her heart.

AUSTIN HAD JUST ZIPPED his suitcase closed when Adam came bouncing into the room. His blond hair was buzzed and flipped in the front. He wore baggy jeans and the Texas Longhorns T-shirt Austin had brought him as a gift.

"Hey, kid, what's going on?"

"Nothin'." Adam leaped onto the bed. "Mom promised to make enchiladas for supper when she gets home from work tonight."

"Your favorite."

"Are you going somewhere, Uncle Austin?"

"I found another place to stay in Seattle."

Adam frowned. "Don't you want to stay with us anymore? I like having you here."

"I like being here, too." Austin sat down on the bed so he could talk to his nephew at eye level. "Can I tell you a secret?"

Adam nodded, scooting closer.

Austin lowered his voice to a whisper. "This houseboat is a great place to live, but it's making me a little seasick."

Adam laughed. "No way."

It was the truth. He'd popped more antacids in the past week than in the past five years. He wondered if Hannah had the same problem. She'd definitely been looking green around the gills lately. "I'm afraid so."

"Maybe you'll get used to it," Adam said hopefully.

Austin shook his head. "I don't think it's something I want to get used to. A cowboy belongs on the land."

"Does my dad know you're leaving?"

"Not yet," Austin replied, wondering if Jack would be relieved. They'd maintained an uneasy alliance since Austin had been staying here, more polite than friendly. Neither one of them seemed able to forget their estrangement over the past decade. But at least they were talking now. "I wanted to wait until…"

But Adam wasn't listening. He ran out into the hallway and shouted, "Dad! Come in here. Hurry!"

Jack was there in an instant. "What's wrong?"

"Uncle Austin is leaving."

Jack relaxed when he realized it wasn't an emergency. His gaze moved from the suitcase on the bed to his brother. "Is this true?"

"I decided to give you three a little space," Austin explained.

"That's not the only reason," Adam said, then clapped one hand over his mouth.

Jack looked curious. "There's another reason?"

"That's a secret," Austin said, winking at Adam.

"What about our deal? I thought you were going to stay in Seattle to help Dana Ulrich plan the wedding."

"The deal's still on, Jack," he assured him, bristling a little that his brother would think he'd go back on his word. "I'm just leaving the houseboat, not Seattle."

"But where will you go? Staying in a hotel will cost you a fortune."

"Actually, I'll be staying with a friend."

The sound of the front door opening made Adam run out into the hallway again. "I'll go tell Mom!"

When his son was gone, Jack turned back to Austin. "Now, tell me what's really going on."

"I'm moving in with Dana."

Jack stared at him for a moment, then shook his head. "Well, hell, that didn't take you long."

"Don't get the wrong idea." Austin held up both hands. "We're just…friends."

"Right," Jack said with a knowing smile.

Hannah appeared in the doorway of the bedroom, Adam right behind her. She looked at Austin, a frown wrinkling her brow. "You're leaving us?"

"He got a better offer," Jack told her.

Austin hauled his suitcase off the bed and handed it to Adam. "Will you take this to my pickup truck for me?"

"Sure," Adam said, half dragging the heavy suitcase out into the hallway.

Hannah walked into the bedroom, placing one slender hand on Austin's arm. "Please don't leave. We like having you here, Austin."

"I'll still be around," he promised her. "I just want to give the three of you more space. You have to admit it's a little crowded."

"And soon to be even more crowded." Hannah smiled as she turned to Jack. "Do you want to tell him or shall I?"

Austin looked from Hannah to his brother. "Tell me what?"

"We're going to have a baby," Jack announced, pride shining in his eyes.

"Wow." Austin reached out to embrace Hannah. "That's terrific."

"Not so fast," she said, laughing. "This baby already makes me feel dizzy."

"So that's why you've looked like hell this past week," Austin said, relief mingled with just the tiniest bit of envy. He'd never seen his brother look so happy.

Hannah laughed. "You do know how to flatter a girl, Austin Hawke."

"Don't underestimate my little brother," Jack told her. "He's been here less than a week and has already found a girl who can't resist him."

Hannah's eyes widened. "Really? Who?"

Austin scowled at his brother. "You could take a lesson from your son in keeping secrets."

"I won't tell anyone," Hannah promised.

"I'm moving in with Dana Ulrich," Austin confided. "But don't read too much into it."

"Our wedding planner?" Hannah asked in amazement.

"And it's all thanks to you," Jack teased her. "Maybe you should forget about day care and set up business as a matchmaker."

"We're not a couple," Austin clarified. "We're just roommates. Hell, I don't think the woman even likes me much." *The way she kissed me told a different story.*

"I find that hard to believe," Hannah said wryly, looking from her fiancé to her future brother-in-law.

"There's something about you cowboys that women find irresistible."

"It's our charm," Jack said.

"Our good looks," Austin added.

"Our warm, engaging personalities," Jack finished, giving his brother a look that took him back ten years.

They were bantering together as if they'd never been apart, Austin realized.

It caught him unawares, and in that moment he realized how much he'd missed having Jack in his life. The ache bit so deep he had to swallow hard to keep from voicing it aloud. He turned to see Hannah watching him, her perceptive gaze flustering him even more.

Austin searched for something to say to get back on solid ground. "So...does Adam know about the baby yet?"

Hannah shook her head. "We want to wait a while before we tell anyone else. I went to my doctor yesterday, and after confirming that I was pregnant, he set up an appointment for me with an obstetrician next week."

"Well, congratulations," Austin reached out to shake his brother's hand.

"Thanks," Jack said, as Adam barreled back into the room.

"Your suitcase is in the truck, Uncle Austin."

"Thanks, kid," Austin said. "Now I just need a hug goodbye."

Adam flew into his arms, laughing as Austin lifted him high off the floor in a big bear hug.

The boy smelled of salt air and cinnamon. For a moment Austin wondered what it would be like to have a son of his own. Someone he could teach to ride and rope. Someone to take over the Hawke Ranch one day.

He set Adam back on the floor, surprised at how hard he found it to leave. "Well, I guess I'd better be on my way."

"You're welcome back anytime," Hannah said as the three of them walked him to the door.

He reached for his cowboy hat hanging on a hook. "I appreciate that."

"'Bye, Uncle Austin."

As he left the houseboat, he looked back to see the three of them framed in the open doorway. The sun's rays reflected off the orange roof, casting a warm glow around their home.

The picture of a perfect family.

Austin walked down the dock until he reached his pickup truck. Funny how he'd never felt this emptiness inside of him until now. Never considered bringing a woman home to the Hawke Ranch.

The idea strangely appealed to him. But it had to be the right woman. Someone who would love the land as much as he did. That put a damper on any wild notions he might be having about a certain city girl.

The problem was that Dana had gotten under his skin. Hell, he'd already kissed her twice. He needed to slow way down before the flames flickering between them roared into a brushfire.

Because Austin didn't want either one of them to get burned.

DANA PACED ACROSS her living room floor, wondering if Austin had changed his mind. He'd left two hours ago, and in that time she'd come up with plenty of reasons why his moving in with her was a really bad idea.

In the first place, he'd already shown a blatant disregard for her rules. What if he got tired of sleeping on the sofa and wanted to move into her bed?

She knew instinctively that Austin would never force himself on her. He had too much of the noble cowboy in him for that. But the sparks between them were too strong for her to ignore. Sure, he might be tall, dark and handsome. A rugged cowboy with a sexy Texas drawl. A superb kisser.

But that didn't make him the right man for her.

She preferred a man of subtlety and sophistication. Someone who didn't overwhelm a room with his sheer physical presence. She'd carefully built her life to mingle in the company of people who enjoyed opera and fine wines. Who listened to National Public Radio, not the Dixie Chicks.

Those were all things to keep in mind the next time she found herself fantasizing about him. She hadn't come this far to backslide now. Besides, Austin would be going back to Texas soon. Right where he belonged.

The doorbell rang and Dana's heart beat doubletime. She smoothed down her dress, then walked to the door, telling herself to play it cool.

But as soon as she opened the door, her resignation faltered. The dim hallway light cast the planes of his face in deep shadows, making him seem even more dangerous and appealing than ever.

She opened the door wider. "Come on in."

He carried a suitcase in one hand and a bedroll in the other. "Where do you want me?"

In Texas. "You'll be sleeping on the sofa," she told him. "But you can store your suitcase and sleeping bag in the hall closet during the day."

He shook his head as he looked at the sofa. "I'll never fit there. If you don't mind, I'll bunk on the floor instead."

"The living room floor?"

Mischievous blue lights danced in his gray eyes. "Do you have someplace better in mind?"

He was purposely trying to bait her. But that didn't mean Dana had to take it. "I thought you might prefer the kitchen. I know how much you like to eat."

His smile made something crackle deep inside of her.

"That's not a bad idea," Austin said, "but if it's all the same to you, I think I'll just camp out here by the fireplace."

"Fine," she said briskly. Moving to the coffee table, she picked up the yellow legal pad and pen that she'd set there earlier. "I think we should schedule a routine so we don't get in each other's way."

Once he'd set his suitcase and bedroll down, he turned to look at her. "This is a small apartment. We're bound to run into each other.

Not if she could help it. "Since you like to get up before sunrise, you can have the shower first. I'll need it by eight o'clock. While I'm in the bathroom, you can eat your breakfast and clear your things out of the living room."

He sat down beside her on the sofa, looking over her shoulder to study the list. She could feel the warm caress of his breath against the nape of her neck.

Dana cleared her throat. "I will answer all incoming

calls, although you're welcome to use the phone for local calls. The only thing I ask is that you not tie up the line for longer than five minutes at a time. I'm trying to run a business here and I need to be available to my clients at all times.''

"What about bedtime?" Austin asked. "Do you have a schedule for that, too?"

She stood up to put some distance between them. "Since you'll be sleeping in the living room, I thought I should leave that up to you. Is there a certain time you like to go to bed?"

"I'm somewhat of a night owl. I don't need much sleep."

"So I won't bother you if I'm up until…say, eleven o'clock?"

"That shouldn't be a problem."

"Good." She set down the notepad. "Then, it's all settled."

"Just one more thing," Austin said, moving closer to her.

She swallowed, tipping her head up to meet his gaze. "Yes?"

"I do all the cooking."

"That's not necessary."

"I insist," he replied. "As you mentioned earlier, I like to eat. I also like to cook. And you're so skinny a strong breeze could blow you away. I want to fatten you up so that doesn't happen before the wedding."

"Fatten me up," she echoed in disbelief. "In case you haven't noticed, Austin, fat is not the newest fad. I'm perfectly healthy for my height and age. I work out regularly in the exercise room downstairs."

He looked surprised. "This building has an exercise room?"

She nodded. "Complete with weight bench, tread-mills, stair-step machines and stationary bicycles. The building also has a sauna, tanning beds, indoor swimming pool, dry-cleaning service, a fax machine and a copier."

"Hell, throw in a grocery store and a person wouldn't even have to step outside."

"I often order my groceries online and have them delivered right to the door." When she had the money to order groceries, that is.

He shook his head. "No wonder so many people in this city look so pale. They never step outside for a breath of fresh air."

"I think that's an exaggeration."

"Maybe," he conceded. "But I still say you're too skinny."

"Since you're not my mother, I'm afraid your opinion doesn't matter." But it did matter—more than she wanted to admit. "I don't want you cooking for me. I can feed myself, thank you very much."

He shrugged. "Then, at least join me in a glass of wine. I bought a bottle to celebrate our first night together."

"Austin," she began, sensing that living with him would definitely be a challenge.

"Our first night together as roommates," he amended. "I've never lived with a woman before. It should be an interesting experience."

She didn't want to admit that she'd never lived with a man, either. Privacy had always been too important to her. And now that privacy was being invaded by a cowboy who wanted to fatten her up!

While he worked in the kitchen, Dana escaped into her bedroom to look at herself in the long mirror. Okay, maybe she had lost a few pounds in the past month or so. That was only natural considering all the stress she'd been under.

She turned to the side to study her profile, then to the front again. Definitely not too skinny. Compared with some of the anorexic supermodels she saw on television, she was downright chubby.

It wasn't as if Austin was perfect, either. Those clothes simply screamed cowboy. His thick black hair was too long, almost touching his shoulders. And he made no effort to polish his country roots, something Dana simply couldn't understand after working so hard to rise above her own upbringing.

Still, he did have a few good points. A nice smile. A fierce, if somewhat annoying, protective streak. A talent in the kitchen. Not bad traits in a roommate.

What Dana found the most intriguing about Austin was his tendency to say exactly what he thought. An inherent honesty that she didn't find much among her friends and associates. Or even in herself. Everyone was so immersed in political correctness that honesty often got pushed to the back burner.

Of course, sometimes honesty could go too far. Like calling her skinny. She was a healthy American girl. And if Austin Hawke didn't like the way she looked, then that was just too bad.

Thirty minutes later, she emerged from her bedroom to be met with a blend of savory aromas. She'd spent that time telling herself not to let Austin's presence affect her usual routine, but her resolve faltered when she walked into the kitchen and saw him pulling a steak from underneath the broiler. A huge skillet of fried potatoes and onions sizzled on the stovetop.

"I made extra, in case you want some."

"Thanks, but I'm really not that hungry," she lied, removing a small carton of yogurt from the refrigerator.

Austin filled his plate at the stove, then sat down at the table across from her. "Do you have any ketchup?"

"I think there's a bottle in the cupboard above the dishwasher."

When he got up to retrieve it, she reached over while his back was turned and snitched a crispy fried potato. Chewing it quickly, she swallowed just as he returned to the table with the ketchup in his hand.

"What have you got there?" he asked, pointing to the carton in front of her.

"Raspberry yogurt."

"I've never eaten yogurt before."

She gaped at him. "Don't they have yogurt in Texas?"

He shrugged. "I'm sure they do, it's just never caught my eye before. Is it good?"

She dipped up a small spoonful and held it out to him. "Try it."

"Only for a fair trade." He stabbed a thick piece of juicy beefsteak with his fork and held it out to her.

She was on to him, but Dana leaned forward and captured the steak with her mouth anyway.

"Good?" he asked.

"Not bad," she replied, resisting the urge to moan

in ecstasy at the taste. Instead, she held out the spoon. "Your turn."

Austin reached out to steady her hand, guiding the spoon to his mouth. His eyes never left her as he wrapped his mouth around the spoon, then slowly slid it off.

"Well?"

He swallowed, then grimaced. "No offense, but that's some of the worst stuff I ever tasted in my life."

"It's very healthy."

"That explains it." He picked up his knife and fork. "In my experience, food that's supposed to be healthy for you usually tastes like crap."

"I happen to like it," she replied, scooping up another spoonful of yogurt.

He leaned back in his chair. "Now tell me the truth. Would you rather eat a carton of yogurt or that extra steak I have over there on the stove?"

"Yogurt."

He grinned. "Liar."

"Red meat is bad for you." She spooned up another bite of yogurt. "It raises your cholesterol."

With a shrug, he turned back to his meal. "Like I said before, stubborn as a mule."

Dana forced her gaze from his steak and finished every last drop of her yogurt. She'd won the battle, though the thought of facing this kind of temptation every day for the next few weeks was almost unbearable.

Maybe Austin would give up before then. But something told her he wasn't the type to surrender easily.

"So, how did you become a wedding planner?" he asked, still working on his steak.

''When I was sixteen, a friend of mine became pregnant,'' Dana began. ''Rachel's boyfriend wanted to marry her, but her family had kicked her out and there was no way either one of them could afford the fairytale wedding she'd always dreamed about. So I offered to help make it come true. I didn't know anything about planning weddings at the time, but they say ignorance is bliss.''

''So Rachel got her fairy-tale wedding?''

She nodded, remembering that special day. The day Dana realized what she wanted to do with the rest of her life. ''The ceremony was in a park in June. Rachel wore my Gram's wedding dress and I'd hocked my stereo to pay for a violinist to provide the music.''

He set down his knife and fork to listen to the rest of her story.

Dana could see that day in her mind. The glow of happiness on her friend's face was something she would never forget. ''Rachel wore a wreath of wildflowers in her hair that I'd picked that morning. The pastor had agreed to waive the fee for performing the ceremony in exchange for my volunteering to paint the church basement.''

''You gave up a lot for her,'' he observed.

''She was a friend,'' Dana said simply. ''I wanted her wedding to be perfect for her.'' She smiled. ''Unfortunately, the wedding cake I baked was a little lopsided, but nobody seemed to mind. Rachel was happy, and that's all that mattered.''

He didn't say anything for a moment, just stared at her in a way that made her think her story had surprised him.

"So you decided to make it a career?" Austin asked at last.

"I'm in the business of making dreams come true," she replied. "I can't think of any job I'd like better."

"I feel the same way about ranching."

"How did you decide to become a cowboy?" she asked, truly curious. Austin struck her as a man who could do anything if he put his mind to it.

"It was more of a legacy than a decision. My great-grandfather settled in Texas over a hundred years ago and built the Hawke Ranch. I guess you could say it's in my blood."

"So you're running the ranch now?"

"I will be if my bank loan comes through."

She didn't want to pry into his financial affairs, especially when she kept her own dire straits so well concealed. "Did you ever consider doing anything else?"

He picked up his fork. "I actually thought about going into medicine for a while, but I love the outdoors too much. So I volunteer on the rural ambulance as an EMT, instead."

Now it was Dana's turn to be surprised. She couldn't picture him as anything but a cowboy. "You're an EMT? Really?"

"Yes, ma'am." He added more pepper to his fried potatoes. "I carry a pager with me all the time back home so I can be ready to go out on a call."

Dana remembered the way he'd taken care of her when she'd almost fainted in his arms. He'd insisted she eat those expensive chocolates until she felt better. "That's how you guessed what was wrong with me the first night we met. You've had some medical training."

"First aid training," he amended, then frowned at the empty yogurt carton in front of her. "Enough to recognize a woman who doesn't eat enough."

She ignored the low rumble in her stomach as she watched him carve into his steak. "I'm fine."

"I guess I'll never understand women," he said, shaking his head. "Endless diets. Wasting money on things like liposuction and expensive cosmetics. Trying to camouflage who they really are when it's what's on the inside that counts."

She stared at him, wondering if he really believed it. "You might want to clue in some of your male counterparts. In case you hadn't noticed, they're the ones who usually prefer beauty over brains."

He smiled. "Okay, I'll admit I may have been guilty of that myself in the past."

"The past?" she challenged. "I thought you told me people couldn't change. So which is it? Beauty or brains?"

"Can I have a third choice?"

"Sure," she said, her curiosity aroused. "I can't wait to hear it."

"Then, I'll take honesty. A woman who isn't afraid to be herself. To say what she really thinks and to go after what she really wants."

Dana wished life could be that easy. Maybe on a ranch in Texas, but here in Seattle it wasn't that simple. A woman had to move in the right circles, say and do the right things to get where she wanted to go. Compromise was part of that equation—like planning

KRISTIN GABRIEL 99

Clark Oxley's wedding. She'd rather tell Clark to go to hell, but she didn't have that luxury.

So Dana would have to smile and pretend everything was all right—a necessary deception if she wanted to keep this job. She knew that made her just the opposite of the kind of woman Austin admired.

Good, she told herself, watching him finish his meal. This cowboy wasn't her type, either. But somewhere deep inside, Dana was beginning to wonder if she was lying to herself.

CHAPTER SIX

AUSTIN AWOKE in the middle of the night to an odd rustling sound in the next room. He lay on the floor in front of the hearth, the red embers still glowing in the grate. Propping up on one elbow, he listened intently in the darkness.

There it was again. A slight creaking sound. Like a footstep.

Rising silently, he moved stealthily toward the kitchen, glancing down the hallway that led to Dana's bedroom. It was dark and the door was still closed. She obviously hadn't been disturbed by the sounds.

He thought about the door off the kitchen that led to the service elevator. Had someone broken in?

Placing one hand on the swinging door, he slowly pushed it open. The kitchen was dark, but he could see a form illuminated in the light of the open refrigerator door.

He flipped the overhead light on. "Gotcha!"

Dana gasped and whirled around, dropping a plastic platter. In her other hand she held a strip of leftover steak from dinner.

Austin grinned. "I caught you red-handed."

Her cheeks turned as pink as the long chenille robe she wore. She stared at him unblinking, her gaze fixed at waist level.

He looked down, realizing too late that he was standing there in his underwear.

"Nice boxer shorts," she said. "I see that contrary to popular opinion, cowboys don't sleep with their boots on."

"We don't make love with our hats on, either. Just in case you were wondering."

"I wasn't," Dana replied, regaining her composure. "What are you doing in here, anyway?"

"I heard a noise and thought it might be a burglar." Then he looked at the steak in her hand. "And I see I was right."

She closed the refrigerator door, bent down to pick up the platter and set it on the counter. "I got a craving."

"Hey, I'm all for midnight cravings." Right now he craved a taste of her. She looked deliciously disheveled with her dark hair askew and the top of the robe gaping open just enough for him to glimpse her tantalizing cleavage. A flash of black lace made him wonder what exactly *she* wore to bed.

"What are you staring at?" she asked, defiantly preparing herself a sandwich with his leftover steak.

"You."

His honesty made her blush deepen. "I think you should go back to bed."

He moved closer, until he could tip up her chin with one finger. Her skin was silky soft, her breath warm on his palm. "You might like me even better than that sandwich."

In response, she raised the sandwich to her mouth and bit off a huge chunk.

He grinned. "Good night, Dana."

Her mouth was too full to respond, so he took advantage of the situation and leaned down to kiss her bulging cheek. "Sweet dreams."

Austin turned around and left before she could lay into him again about breaking one of her rules. He didn't want her to see the condition she'd put him in, one that was all too apparent, considering his attire.

Settling back down on the floor, Austin pulled the blanket up around his shoulders, trying to get comfortable again. But sleep eluded him and he knew the reason was more than physical. He had tried to peg Dana as a shallow, self-absorbed city girl, but the story she'd told him tonight about planning her friend's wedding made him realize he'd read her all wrong.

He should have realized it even sooner, when she'd confessed to him that she'd been called a trailer-trash tramp in high school. *Trailer trash.* Did that mean she hadn't always lived in such posh surroundings? Watching her with Clark and Alison this evening, he'd sensed a steel underneath that creamy, lush surface. A survival instinct that appealed to him.

The more he got to know her, the more Dana intrigued him. Enticed him. He'd wished her sweet dreams, but Austin had no doubt he'd lay awake all night fantasizing about how sweet she'd taste in his arms.

THE NEXT MORNING, Dana managed to avoid Austin by slipping out of the apartment while he was in the shower. She didn't know which bothered her more—that he'd caught her pilfering his steak or that he'd done it in his underwear.

Not that he'd seemed embarrassed about it. Did

nothing faze that man? She could still picture him standing there—the breadth of his broad, muscular chest layered with fine, dark hair. The taut, washboard ripples across his stomach. Not to mention the impressive bulge beneath the thin cotton of his blue boxers.

Just thinking about it made her feel a little breathless. She couldn't remember the last time she'd had an almost naked man in her kitchen. Especially a man of such…proportions.

"Nothing happened," Dana reminded herself as she drove toward Forrester Square Day Care.

She had a full day planned with Hannah and her bridesmaids. First, they were meeting for breakfast at Caffeine Hy's, next to the day care, then on to the Smith Tower to shop for the two bridesmaids' dresses, shoes and other accessories.

With Hannah along for the trip, Dana didn't have to worry about gaining Austin's approval for this purchasing decision. How could she ever face him again without thinking about how he looked without his clothes on?

"Just get over it," she chastised herself, pulling in to a parking lot adjacent to the day care. Then she got out of her car and looked up at the place she'd heard Hannah mention so often.

A huge banner in the shape of a house hung from the roof of the sandstone building. The words Forrester Square Day Care were written in bright, childlike lettering. Three stories tall, the building was surrounded by a wrought-iron fence. As she rounded the parking lot and headed toward the front entrance, Dana could glimpse playground equipment at the rear of the building.

Since it was Saturday, the day care wasn't operating, but as Dana walked inside, she could imagine the sound of children singing and chatting.

Hannah appeared in the office doorway and waved her inside. "Hi, Dana, you're right on time. Unfortunately, Alexandra and Katherine are both running a little late."

"No problem," Dana assured her. "I don't have any other appointments today, so my time is yours."

"Wonderful," Hannah exclaimed. "Would you like a tour of the place?"

"I'd love one."

Hannah led her directly across the hall. "This is our five- and six-year-old room."

A middle-aged woman with short black hair that was graying at the temples walked over to them.

"This is Dana Ulrich," Hannah told the woman. "My wedding planner. Dana, this is Carmen Perez, our head teacher. Carmen insisted on coming in today to sort a new shipment of books that arrived yesterday."

Smiling, Carmen reached out to squeeze both of Dana's hands in her own. "A wedding planner! What a wonderful career."

"I enjoy it," Dana replied, warming to the woman instantly. She had a sunny, grandmotherly air about her.

"I love weddings," Carmen declared. "Almost as much as I love children." Then she turned to Hannah. "Amy was here earlier with the baby. She was shopping in the area. Did you see her?"

"No," Hannah replied, sounding disappointed. "I missed her."

"Leanne is such a little darling," Carmen said.

"Amy Tidwell is one of our aides," Hannah told Dana. "She just had a baby last month, so she isn't back to work yet."

"She's only eighteen," Carmen added. "But a very sweet girl. She's had a tough time of it." Then she looked at Hannah. "I'm so glad you're letting Amy and the baby stay in your apartment. She needed a break from her father, and her other living arrangements just weren't working out."

"I was glad to do it," Hannah replied. "Now that I'm living with Jack and Adam on the houseboat, it seemed like the perfect solution."

Hannah and Dana left Carmen to her sorting and continued the tour.

"We're so lucky to have Carmen," Hannah said. "She actually owned this building before it became Forrester Square Day Care. Katherine met her at the wedding of one of Carmen's sons and they hit it off immediately. When Katherine offered to buy the building, she offered Carmen a job as well. Carmen taught school for almost thirty years, so her experience is invaluable to us."

"She seems very happy here."

"I think she is. Carmen's a widow, and with her four sons all married and starting families of their own, she was ready for some new challenges in her life." Hannah laughed. "And believe me, some days it can be *very* challenging around here."

"But you love it," she observed, recognizing the

enthusiasm in Hannah's voice that Dana had for her own career.

"I do," Hannah concurred as she led Dana down the hallway. "This is our events room, where we hold story hour. And at the end of the hall is the classroom for the four-year-olds."

Dana couldn't help but be impressed by the warmth and cheerfulness she found here. Everything was neatly organized and virtually spotless.

"The kitchen and dining area are across the hall," Hannah said, pointing them out to her. "Snack time is pretty popular around here."

When they reached the second floor, Hannah pointed out the nursery and the toddlers' rooms, as well as a room for the day care's nurse.

"I've saved the best for last," Hannah said as she opened the door in front of her. "This is my favorite room."

Dana walked inside to see cribs lining each wall, a cuddly toy and colorful mobile in each one. Her heart melted at the sight.

"What a lovely nursery," Dana said.

"I know," Hannah agreed as they exited the room. "I come up here all the time."

Seeing the nursery reminded Dana how much she wanted a family—someday. Only, it seemed that day kept getting pushed farther and farther away. She was twenty-eight, with no marital prospect on the horizon.

Austin popped into her mind, but she quickly shoved him out again. She might be attracted to the man, but that didn't make him husband material. Dana believed the kind of man she wanted, the kind of life she wanted, could only be found in the city. Not on some wide Texas prairie.

"Here comes Alexandra," Hannah said, breaking her reverie.

Dana looked up to see a petite redhead bustling toward them. She was naturally pretty, with fair, flawless skin and moss-green eyes. She moved with a restless energy that brought color to her cheeks and explained why there was little fat on her small, wiry frame.

Hannah made the introductions.

"I've heard so many good things about you," Alexandra said, shaking Dana's hand.

Dana recalled what reporter Debbie North had told her about Alexandra Webber. How the woman's parents had been killed in a house fire when she was only six years old.

She wondered if a person ever really got over something like that. Obviously, Alexandra had moved on with her life, reuniting with her two old friends and building a business with them.

"Are we ready to go to Caffeine Hy's?" Hannah asked, walking toward the staircase.

"I just wanted to tell you that Katherine called," Alexandra informed them, "and she and Carlos are going to meet us at the Smith Tower. Carlos is coming with us. But don't worry," she added with a laugh. "He wouldn't be caught dead in a bridal shop! He'll be meeting one of his friends at the arcade."

Hannah turned to Dana. "Carlos is Katherine's foster son. He's only twelve, but when he grows up he's going to be a real lady-killer."

An hour later, Dana agreed with Hannah's prediction. Carlos Vega was tall and gangly, but with his dark hair and eyes, he was already a preteen heart-throb. He attracted packs of young girls as he walked with the four women among the shops in the Smith Tower.

Katherine checked her watch. "Looks like we're a little early, Carlos. Your friend Tony won't be at the arcade for another twenty minutes."

A mischievous twinkle lit his eyes. "Then, that gives us just enough time to visit the Chinese Room."

Katherine sighed. "Now, we already talked about this, Carlos. I'm not sitting in the Wishing Chair. I don't believe in that mystical mumbo jumbo."

Dana had heard about the Wishing Chair, though she'd never actually seen it before. According to legend, a woman who sat in the chair was destined to marry within a year. No doubt many single women had made pilgrimages there, but Dana had never been quite that desperate.

Now it seemed Carlos was determined to play matchmaker for his foster mother.

"How about democracy?" he asked. "Do you believe in that? Because we've been studying it in school."

She looked taken aback by his question. "Of course I believe in democracy."

Carlos turned to the rest of the group. "Okay, everybody who wants Katherine to sit in the Wishing Chair, raise your hand."

Hannah, Alexandra and Dana all raised their hands with Carlos.

"Looks like you're outvoted," he crowed.

Katherine laughed, then reached out to ruffle his

hair. "All right, you win. *This time*. At least I know you're paying attention in class."

As they rode up the hand-operated brass elevator to the Chinese Room on the thirty-fifth floor, Dana mentally checked off the items on her to-do list for Hannah and Jack's wedding. They would shop for the bridesmaids' dresses this morning, then she and Austin would go to the bakery this afternoon to make a final decision on a wedding cake. They still needed to select flowers, a caterer and, most important of all, a place to hold the ceremony and reception.

"Thirty-fifth floor," the elevator operator announced.

Carlos practically dragged Katherine into the Chinese Room.

Dana entered more slowly, awed by the beauty of the hand-carved wood and porcelain inlay ceiling overhead. The room was filled with ornate blackwood furniture and seventeenth-century art.

"There it is," Carlos cried, pointing out the Wishing Chair.

Images of a dragon and a phoenix were hewn into the elaborately carved blackwood of the Wishing Chair. Dana had never been the superstitious type, but even she felt an odd flutter of excitement when Katherine sat gingerly in the chair.

"This is silly," Katherine said, her cheeks flushed.

Alexandra moved to read the small placard on the wall. "Legend says that if you wish for your dream lover while sitting in this chair, you will find him."

"True love isn't magical," Katherine replied, shifting uncomfortably in the chair.

''Maybe you should close your eyes,'' Carlos suggested.

''And stop being such a skeptic,'' Hannah teased.

Katherine closed her eyes with a sigh. A moment later she opened them again. ''Am I still single?''

Carlos laughed. ''Yes, but not for long!''

''Now it's someone else's turn,'' Katherine said, getting out of the chair.

''I've already got my dream man,'' Hannah replied with a smile.

''And I've got Griffin Frazier,'' Alexandra said. ''I'm not sure he's my dream man, but I'm quite happy with the status quo.''

Katherine turned to Dana. ''Are you dating someone, too?''

''Well…'' Dana wasn't quite sure how to describe her relationship with Austin. She could see Hannah looking quizzically at her. ''Sort of.''

''Not good enough,'' Katherine said, propelling her into the chair.

''Now close your eyes,'' Katherine ordered. ''I can't be the only one who looks ridiculous today.''

With a sigh of resignation, Dana closed her eyes. Unbidden, an image of Austin came into her head. The Austin she'd seen last night, all hard muscle and bare skin. Her breath caught in her throat and her eyes flew open.

She shot out of the chair. ''That's enough for me.''

As the others perused the art and furniture in the Chinese Room, Dana took a moment by herself to calm down. The Wishing Chair was just a silly superstition. It didn't mean anything. She knew Austin was all wrong for her. Anybody could see that.

So why was her heart still resounding like a gong in her chest?

"Too much caffeine," she muttered to herself as she rejoined the group. That had to be it. From now on, no more double lattes.

They dropped Carlos off at the arcade, then the women embarked on their search for the perfect bridesmaid's dress. Dana knew it wouldn't be easy finding something to flatter both of Hannah's bridesmaids. Katherine was four inches taller and about twenty pounds heavier than Alexandra.

But two hours later, they were successful.

"I love the color," Alexandra said as they walked out of La Boutique, an exclusive shop that specialized in designer wedding apparel.

Katherine nodded in agreement. "I always thought coral would make me look washed out, but it's perfect."

"I'll let you know when La Boutique is ready for you to come in for the second fitting," Dana said. "Probably sometime next week."

"Where did Hannah go?" Alexandra asked, looking around the mall.

"She went in search of the ladies' room while you two were in the dressing room changing out of the gowns," Dana replied. "I don't think she was feeling very well."

Katherine and Alexandra exchanged concerned glances. Then Alexandra said, "I'll go find her."

After she left, Katherine started digging in her tote bag. "Hey, I've got some brochures that might interest you, Dana. Hannah said you're in charge of finding a place for the wedding ceremony. I collect travel brochures and have a ton from the Seattle area.''

"I'd love to see them," Dana said, willing to take help wherever she could find it.

"I know I have those brochures in here somewhere," Katherine muttered, sitting down on a nearby bench. "Here they are." She pulled out a thick stack and handed them to Dana.

"Thanks," she said, looking at the top brochure. "The Lord Mansion."

"That's in Olympia," Katherine said.

"I think Hannah and Jack are pretty set on getting married in Seattle." Dana started flipping through the other brochures. "The Sercombe House. Salish Lodge. Heron Beach Inn. These all look wonderful."

"Take a look at the one for the Sorrento Hotel. I think that is such a romantic spot for a wedding. Carmen's son Rick was married there last year."

"Hey, this one looks interesting," Dana said, flipping over the next brochure. "The Windmere Center. I don't think I've ever heard of it."

When Katherine didn't say anything, Dana looked up to see the woman's face turn bright red.

Then Katherine cleared her throat. "I'm positive Hannah and Jack do not want the wedding ceremony there."

"Why not?" Dana asked, opening the brochure.

Katherine closed her eyes. "Because it's a sperm bank."

Dana saw dancing test tubes on the inside of the brochure. "A sperm bank?"

With a sigh, Katherine opened her eyes. "It must

have gotten mixed up with the other brochures. I'm so sorry.''

"No, I'm sorry," Dana said, handing it back to her. "I didn't mean to embarrass you."

"It's not your fault," Katherine assured her. "It's the fault of my biological clock. I'm going to be thirty soon, and the ticking is growing louder by the day. But please don't tell anyone about that brochure. I'm not even sure I'll go through with it."

"I won't say a word," Dana promised. "To tell you the truth, I've started wondering myself what I'll do if I still haven't found Mr. Right when I reach my thirties. I know I want children...."

"Me, too," Katherine replied. "Taking care of Carlos has made that even clearer to me."

"He talked you into sitting in the Wishing Chair," Dana reminded her, "so, according to legend, you should be married within a year."

Katherine smiled. "I promise you can be my wedding planner if I do."

"I'm going to hold you to that," Dana said, laughing as Hannah and Alexandra reappeared.

"Although, you might be too busy planning your own wedding." Katherine rose from the bench. "We'll both be getting married if there's any truth to that legend. At least you already have a boyfriend. I'm not even dating anyone."

Dana almost confided that her boyfriend wasn't real. The problem was that living with Austin almost made it seem real. Or maybe that was just wishful thinking. She'd spent most of last night fantasizing about the man sleeping in the next room.

As they left the Smith Tower to go their separate

ways, Dana told herself those fantasies had to stay in her head. Despite her wild flight of imagination in the Wishing Chair, there'd be no wedding for her—at least, not with Austin Hawke as her groom.

CHAPTER SEVEN

"AM I DOING IT RIGHT, Uncle Austin?" Adam asked, swinging the lasso around his head.

"Looks good to me." Austin stood on the dock beside his nephew. He'd been recruited to baby-sit while Jack took Hannah to her first appointment with her new obstetrician. "Now, keep your shoulder loose, and when you toss it, let the momentum of the rope carry it to the pole."

Adam twirled the lasso a few more times, then let it fly, aiming for the weathered post at the end of the dock. The lasso fell about five feet short.

"Good try," Austin said.

Adam grimaced. "I missed again."

"Hey, it takes a lot of practice."

"Yeah, but I can't even rope a post that's standing still. You can rope cows while riding on a horse." He squinted up at him. "Dad said you got a trophy once for roping."

"That was a long time ago." He couldn't believe Jack remembered that far back. Austin had only been sixteen at the time and had gone up against older cowboys with a lot more experience. But with some luck and a few good tips from his big brother, he'd managed to beat all the competition that day. Not that his father had cared. Or even noticed.

Adam dragged the lasso back toward him. "Show me how to do it one more time."

Austin took the rope from him, coiling up the free end and holding it in his left hand. Then he grasped the lasso end just below the knot and began spinning it. When it reached the right velocity, he tossed the lasso toward the post. The lasso looped around the top, and he pulled on the rope to secure it.

"Yes!" Adam exclaimed, pumping his fist in the air. "You did it!"

"I tamed a wild post," Austin teased, then heard the sound of clapping behind him and turned around to see his brother and Hannah walking up the dock toward them.

"I hope you're not trying to lure our son into the cowboy life," Jack said.

"He's got some natural talent." Austin ruffled Adam's hair. "I could use a good hand like him back on the ranch."

"Really?" Adam said, his blue eyes widening.

"Maybe when you're a little older, you can spend a couple of weeks on the ranch during the summer," Jack said, looking at his fiancée. "What do you think?"

Hannah blinked, then looked up at him. "I'm sorry. What did you say?"

Austin could tell something was wrong. Hannah looked pale and her mind was obviously elsewhere.

Jack leaned over to kiss her cheek. "Adam might spend a couple of weeks in Texas sometime, but we can talk about it later."

She gave a slight nod, then turned toward the houseboat, walking inside without another word.

"What's wrong with Mom?" Adam asked.

"She's just tired," Jack replied, staring after her.

"She's *always* tired," Adam said, then turned to his uncle. "Can I try it again?"

"Sure." Austin handed him the rope, then followed Jack to the deck chairs to watch. Gulls flew overhead, and several boaters were out on the lake, enjoying the unusually balmy day.

Austin sensed a tension in Jack that he hadn't noticed before Hannah's appointment. Something had obviously gone wrong at the doctor's office. He sat back in the chair, not wanting to pry. They watched in silence as Adam struggled with the lasso.

"My son reminds me a little of you," Jack said at last. "Determined not to give up until he does it right."

"Funny, I was just about to say the same thing about you. Maybe that's why Hannah calls us both stubborn. Must be a genetic trait, after all."

"Looks like Adam inherited it," Jack mused. "No doubt the new baby will, too."

Austin hesitated. "So, is everything all right? With the baby, I mean.'

Jack nodded. "The baby is fine and Hannah's in good health. She's about six weeks along and the obstetrician doesn't anticipate any problems."

"But something has upset her," Austin observed.

His brother sighed. "It was something the nurse said. As a new patient, they needed Hannah's medical history—including her blood type."

"How is that a problem?"

"Because Hannah told the nurse she already knew her blood type was A positive. She explained that both she and her mother were tested when her father was in that car accident to see if they matched his A negative blood. But neither one did. Olivia was B negative. Before the test results came back, the hospital discovered Hannah was pregnant and she was told that prevented her from donating blood, regardless of the test results."

"Wait, something doesn't sound right," Austin replied, thinking of his medical training. As an EMT, he'd been thoroughly educated on the complexities of blood types and compatibility.

"That's what the nurse said when Hannah told her the story." Jack shook his head. "The woman just wouldn't let it go. She insisted that if Hannah was type A positive, she cannot be the biological child of parents who both have a negative blood and RH factor."

"No, she can't," Austin murmured, considering all the implications.

"The nurse even asked her if she was adopted."

Austin shook his head. "What was that nurse thinking? Didn't she realize how this kind of information would affect Hannah?"

"I don't know," Jack replied tightly. "When I complained to the doctor, he said she was new, just out of nursing school, and that he'd have a talk with her. Not that it will matter to Hannah now. She's still in shock. I tried to tell her those blood tests could have been wrong. That even if they weren't wrong, it didn't really matter. Kenneth and Olivia raised her and loved her. They're her real parents."

"And?"

"And she's too upset to listen. Hannah's starting to

question everything about her past now, including why her parents got divorced.''

"Why did they?"

Jack shrugged. ''I always assumed they just grew apart. Olivia divorced him back in 1984, and neither one of them has ever remarried. They're both well-off and seem cordial enough with one another.''

"And Hannah's stayed close to both of them?''

"For the most part. I think that's why this is so difficult for her. She doesn't know if they lied to her or lied to each other.'' Jack clenched his jaw. ''All I know is that this is the last thing Hannah needs right now.''

"You'll get her through this, Jack,'' Austin said. "You and Adam and the baby.''

"I hope so.'' Jack turned to his brother, hesitating a moment before he spoke. ''I've got to tell you, I wasn't too thrilled when Hannah asked you to stick around Seattle and help plan our wedding.''

"Neither was I,'' Austin admitted.

"But now, I'm glad you're here,'' he said awkwardly. ''Hannah really doesn't need any wedding stress on top of all this. I just wanted you to know…I appreciate the help.''

The words didn't come easily to Jack, which made them all the more powerful to Austin. For the first time since he'd arrived in Seattle, he truly felt like part of their family. ''I'll do whatever I can.''

"Just keep Dana Ulrich in line,'' Jack said. ''I want this wedding to go off without a hitch.''

"Dana knows what she's doing,'' he said, a little too defensively.

Jack arched a brow. ''So you two are hitting it off?''

Austin wasn't sure how to answer him. The more time he spent with Dana, the more he liked her. Even if the woman did drive him crazy at times. He had no doubt the feeling was mutual. Yet she still seemed skittish around him.

"What makes you think she'd be interested in a cowboy?" he hedged.

"You haven't lost your touch with roping," Jack said, "so don't tell me you've lost it with women."

Austin honestly didn't know. But maybe it was time to find out.

THREE DAYS LATER, Hannah awaited her mother at the Athenian Inn restaurant in Pike Place Market. She sat at a table by a window, able to see the fish jugglers entertaining people on the sidewalk. This was her favorite place in Seattle. It was the site of the oldest continuous farmers' market in the country, set amid a labyrinth of restaurants and antique shops.

Hannah usually enjoyed the shouts and banter of farmers and fishermen as colorful as their produce. But today was different. All she could think about was how to ask her mother the questions that had been burning inside of her since that visit to the obstetrician.

Jack wanted her to just let it go, concerned that she was already stressed enough with running the day care, the upcoming wedding and her pregnancy. But those were all *good* things. This sudden revelation about the incompatible blood types had been haunting her day and night.

She looked away from the window to see her mother entering the restaurant. People often said Olivia Richards didn't look old enough to have a twenty-eight-year-old daughter. Now Hannah tried to look at her mother objectively, seeing her as a stranger might.

Thin and fit, the fifty-six-year-old took impeccable care of herself. She worked out religiously in order to wear the expensive designer clothes she loved so much. And though her perfect skin owed a small debt to plastic surgery, the only other artifice about her was her light brown hair touched with golden highlights, which came out of a bottle.

Olivia had brown eyes, while her own were light blue. Her father had brown eyes, too. Hannah could remember remarking on it once as a child, wondering why she had blue eyes when her parents both had brown. Olivia had pointed to a picture of her own mother, who had eyes like the summer sky, and said those blue eyes must have skipped a generation.

Hannah had believed her explanation. Why wouldn't she? But now she feared there was another one.

"Hello, darling." Olivia leaned over the table and brushed an air kiss across Hannah's cheek.

"Hi, Mom," she replied, suddenly wishing she'd picked a different restaurant. Hannah usually loved the fragrant aroma of Greek food, but her stomach was too sensitive to handle it today.

Or maybe it was nerves. She'd told herself not to bring up the subject of the blood types, since they'd planned this lunch together weeks ago to talk about the wedding. But how could she avoid it?

Olivia took the chair across from her. "Where is your wedding planner?"

"Dana's running a little late," Hannah informed

her. "She called to say she'd be here in about twenty minutes."

"Good." Olivia signaled the waiter. "That gives us some time alone together. You're so busy these days, I hardly get to see you anymore."

"I have a family now," Hannah replied, "as well as my position at the day care."

The waiter arrived and Olivia ordered a glass of ouzo. "Care to join me?" she asked her daughter.

"I'll just have sparkling water with a twist of lime," Hannah told the waiter.

"We should really be ordering champagne," Olivia said after the waiter walked away. "You're getting married. This is a time to celebrate."

"In more ways than one." Hannah took a deep breath. "I'm pregnant."

Olivia blanched. "Pregnant? Are you sure?"

She nodded. "I saw an obstetrician a few days ago. He told me I'm about six weeks along."

"Well, dear..." Olivia hesitated, as if uncertain whether to offer congratulations or condolences. "How do you feel about it?"

"Jack and I are both thrilled," Hannah assured her.

"Then, so am I." Olivia reached across the table to squeeze her daughter's hand, the sunlight catching the ruby-and-diamond ring she always wore. "I just hope you won't be showing at the wedding."

"I'll only be three months along. When I was pregnant with Adam, I didn't start showing until almost six months."

"I'm sure you weren't taking proper care of yourself," Olivia scolded.

"It was a difficult time," Hannah reminded her. "I

was single and pregnant, thinking Jack had abandoned me. Dad had been severely injured in that car crash and was in the hospital for weeks.''

Olivia sighed. ''I know.''

''I remember the nurse mentioning that the blood bank was low on Dad's blood type, A negative,'' Hannah continued, creating an opening. ''They were asking family members to donate blood.''

''That's an odd thing to remember. It was such a long time ago.''

The waiter appeared with their drinks and set them on the table. ''Are you ready to order now?''

''We're waiting for someone,'' Olivia told him. ''Give us about twenty minutes.''

''Very good, ma'am.''

Olivia took a sip of her drink. ''I think we should talk about happier times.''

But Hannah couldn't let the subject go yet. ''You didn't donate blood.''

A slight frown ruffled her mother's smooth forehead. ''Yes, because I was type B negative. Otherwise, I would have been happy to donate blood to your father. I assume when they found out you were pregnant, they wouldn't let you donate, either.''

''That's right. But they tested me before they knew I was pregnant. That's how I found out I'm type A positive.''

''Hannah, what's gotten into you today?'' Olivia asked. ''You seem positively maudlin with all this blood talk.''

She took a deep breath; having gone too far to turn back now. ''I've recently learned that parents who both have negative blood types can't possibly have a child with a positive blood type."

Olivia's mouth tightened. "I'm not sure I understand what you're trying to say."

It seemed obvious to Hannah. "Is there something you haven't told me? Am I adopted or…"

"Or what?" Olivia said sharply.

"I don't know. I'm just trying to make sense of all this."

"Don't be ridiculous. There is a simple explanation," Olivia assured her. "Either the doctor is wrong, or that blood bank was wrong when it tested both of us ten years ago. It's always so hectic in those places. I'm sure that's what happened."

"Maybe you're right," Hannah conceded, though she wasn't convinced. "Would you be willing to have your blood type tested again?"

"Absolutely not," Olivia said, seemingly affronted that she'd even been asked. "This is silly, Hannah. You are my daughter. I gave birth to you, and unfortunately, I still have the stretch marks to prove it."

Feeling almost worse than she had before, Hannah fell silent.

Olivia leaned forward, her tone gentler now. "Darling, medical labs make mistakes all the time. That's why malpractice insurance and health costs are sky high—because of all the lawsuits."

Hannah wished she could take comfort in her mother's easy dismissal of the matter, but it still gnawed at her. "You won't take another test, just so we can be sure?"

"I'm already sure," Olivia said firmly. "Besides, I hate needles. You know they make me faint."

"No, I didn't know that."

"Well, they do. That's why I never go in for a flu shot or a tetanus shot." She picked up her glass and smiled over the rim. "I like to live dangerously."

Dana arrived before Hannah could pursue the topic any further.

"Sorry I'm late," Dana said, slightly breathless as she sat down in the empty chair.

"You're right on time," Olivia replied, holding out one slender hand. "You must be the wedding planner. I'm Olivia Richards, the mother of the bride."

"So nice to meet you," Dana said, noting that Hannah looked a little upset. Something told her she'd come at a bad time, though neither woman asked her to leave. In fact, Olivia seemed quite happy to see her.

"I can't wait to hear all the details about the wedding," Olivia said. "It's not every day that your little girl gets married."

"Shall we order first?" Hannah suggested, her voice oddly subdued.

"Certainly, dear," Olivia said, reaching for the menu beside her.

Dana studied her own menu, then glanced at Hannah and Olivia over the top of it, sensing the tension between them. Of course, weddings could be stressful for the bride's family, so it might be nothing to worry about. Still, with Dana's recently dismal success rate, she hoped it was nothing serious.

After they placed their orders, Olivia turned to Dana. "Do you have any idea where I might find a mother of the bride dress that isn't one of those hideous sequin-and-lace monstrosities you see in all the bridal magazines? I want something with style."

Dana could see by the clothes Olivia wore that she had expensive taste. "Have you ever shopped at La Boutique in the Smith Tower? Marco Kahn has some wonderful original designs there in both formal wear and wedding gowns."

"Marco Kahn?" Olivia tapped her chin with her index finger. "I'm not sure I've heard of him. He's a new designer?"

"Fairly new," Dana replied. "He just moved to Europe a few months ago, though he's originally from Seattle. His designs are now sold worldwide."

"He designed the wedding gown I'm going to wear," Hannah added.

"You've already picked one out?" Olivia's mouth turned down in a frown. "I wanted to help you, darling. To find the perfect dress for you."

"It is perfect," her daughter assured her. "Katherine and Alexandra were with me when I chose it."

"So, what does it look like?" Olivia asked.

"It's ivory and worn off the shoulders." As Hannah described her bridal gown, her face grew animated. "And it has a beaded empire bodice and satin organza skirt. It makes me feel like a princess."

Olivia's eyes misted. "It sounds lovely."

"Dana recommended this particular dress," Hannah told her. "And when I tried it on, I just knew it was meant to be my wedding gown."

"Then, I will definitely check out La Boutique," Olivia said with a perfect French accent. "But perhaps I should know what Jack's mother is planning to wear to the wedding before I choose my dress."

Hannah gaped at her. "Mom, I know I've told you

that Jack lost his mother in a car accident when he was sixteen.''

"Oh, that's right," Olivia said, "you did tell me." She shook her head. "How tragic.''

Hannah sighed. "It really was. Austin was only twelve at the time. I think Jack tried to take him under his wing, but they were both devastated.''

Dana's heart ached for the little boy she imagined Austin had once been. How he'd been forced to grow up in a hurry. Maybe that explained his impatience with some of the luxurious trappings of city life. He'd learned the ugly realities of life at an early age.

"It's no wonder those boys turned out so wild," Olivia said, "without a mother to guide them.''

"They seem to be all right now," Dana chimed in, finding herself coming to Austin's defense. "Jack is a parole officer and Austin will soon be taking over his father's ranch back in Texas.''

"Let's just hope he doesn't follow in his father's footsteps." Olivia took a sip of her ouzo. "Hannah told me Lincoln Hawke was a nasty drunk.''

"Austin is nothing like his father," Hannah said, bristling a little. "He may have a few rough edges, but who wouldn't, with the kind of life he had? I think he's a good man.''

"I never said he wasn't," Olivia countered. "I don't even know the man, other than what you've told me about him. Haven't he and Jack been estranged for years?''

"Yes, but they've reconciled," Hannah said. "In fact, Austin is helping Dana plan the wedding.''

"Darling, don't sound so defensive." Olivia set down her glass. "I'm happy that Jack has his half brother back in his life. Perhaps Austin will even move to Seattle someday to be closer to his family. I certainly can't imagine why anyone would want to live in the wilds of Texas."

"The Hawke Ranch is only about thirty minutes from Dallas," Hannah informed her. "So it's not exactly isolated from civilization."

"It's still a ranch," Olivia said with a shudder. "With dust and cattle and flies. I'd go crazy."

Dana wondered if she would, as well. Although, after living in the close confines of a trailer park, then in an apartment building with so many strangers, she found the possibility of all that privacy appealing to her. Austin obviously loved it. You could hear it in his voice and see it in his eyes every time he talked about his ranch.

"You just don't like the outdoors," Hannah told her mother, laying her napkin in her lap. "Remember how much you used to dread sailing with Dad?"

"Only because he insisted we go every weekend," Olivia said with a groan. "I think he'd live in that sailboat if he could. He used to spend more time at the Harbor Club than at home."

Dana looked up from her plate. "He's a member of the Harbor Club?"

Hannah nodded. "He has been for years. Why?"

"Have you ever thought of holding your wedding and reception there? It's certainly big enough for the number of guests you have planned. And if your father's a member, we shouldn't have any trouble getting it reserved."

"You're right." Hannah looked over at her mother. "What do you think?"

An Important Message from the Editors

Dear Reader,

Because you've chosen to read one of our fine romance novels, we'd like to say "thank you!" And, as a **special** way to thank you, we've selected <u>two more</u> of the books you love so well **plus** an exciting Mystery Gift to send you— absolutely <u>FREE</u>!

Please enjoy them with our compliments...

Pam Powers

Lift here

Peel off seal and place inside...

How to validate your Editor's
"Thank You"
FREE GIFT

1. Peel off gift seal from front cover. Place it in space provided at right. This automatically entitles you to receive 2 FREE BOOKS and a fabulous mystery gift.

2. Send back this card and you'll get 2 brand-new *Romance* novels. These books have a cover price of $5.99 or more each in the U.S. and $6.99 or more each in Canada, but they are yours to keep absolutely free.

3. There's no catch. You're under no obligation to buy anything. We charge nothing—ZERO—for your first shipment. And you don't have to make any minimum number of purchases— not even one!

4. The fact is, thousands of readers enjoy receiving their books by mail from The Reader Service. They enjoy the convenience of home delivery...they like getting the best new novels at discount prices BEFORE they're available in stores... and they love their Heart to Heart subscriber newsletter featuring author news, horoscopes, recipes, book reviews and much more!

5. We hope that after receiving your free books you'll want to remain a subscriber. But the choice is yours— to continue or cancel, any time at all! So why not take us up on our invitation, with no risk of any kind. You'll be glad you did!

GET A *Free* MYSTERY GIFT...

*SURPRISE MYSTERY GIFT COULD BE YOURS **FREE** AS A SPECIAL "THANK YOU" FROM THE EDITORS*

The Editor's "Thank You" Free Gifts Include:

- *Two BRAND-NEW Romance novels!*
- *An exciting mystery gift!*

Yes! I have placed my
Editor's "Thank You" seal in the
space provided above. Please
send me 2 free books and a
fabulous mystery gift. I
understand I am under no
obligation to purchase any
books, as explained on the
back and on the opposite page.

PLACE
FREE GIFT
SEAL
HERE

393 MDL DVFG   193 MDL DVFF

FIRST NAME	LAST NAME

ADDRESS

APT.#	CITY

STATE/PROV.   ZIP/POSTAL CODE

(PR-R-04)

Thank You!

▼ DETACH AND MAIL CARD TODAY! ▼

The Reader Service — Here's How It Works:

Accepting your 2 free books and gift places you under no obligation to buy anything. You may keep the books and gift and return the shipping statement marked "cancel." If you do not cancel, about a month later we'll send you 3 additional books and bill you just $4.74 each in the U.S., or $5.24 each in Canada, plus 25¢ shipping & handling per book and applicable taxes if any.* That's the complete price and — compared to cover prices starting from $5.99 each in the U.S. and $6.99 each in Canada — it's quite a bargain! You may cancel at any time, but if you choose to continue, every month we'll send you 3 more books, which you may either purchase at the discount price or return to us and cancel your subscription.

*Terms and prices subject to change without notice. Sales tax applicable in N.Y. Canadian residents will be charged applicable provincial taxes and GST.

If offer card is missing write to: The Reader Service, 3010 Walden Ave., P.O. Box 1867, Buffalo, NY 14240-1867.

BUSINESS REPLY MAIL

FIRST-CLASS MAIL   PERMIT NO. 717-003   BUFFALO, NY

POSTAGE WILL BE PAID BY ADDRESSEE

THE READER SERVICE
3010 WALDEN AVE
PO BOX 1341
BUFFALO NY 14240-8571

NO POSTAGE
NECESSARY
IF MAILED
IN THE
UNITED STATES

"I think it would be perfect," Olivia concurred. "They have valet parking and a wonderful chef. And the view would be spectacular."

Hannah nodded. "The more I think about it, the more I like it."

"I could check into it and let you know if they have that weekend in April available," Dana offered.

"That sounds great. Why don't you and Austin come over for dinner tomorrow night so we can discuss it?"

"Tomorrow is Valentine's Day," Olivia reminded her daughter. "Aren't you going to do something romantic with Jack?"

Hannah smiled. "Staying home with Jack and my son sounds romantic enough to me."

"I'm afraid Austin and I have plans, though," Dana said. "We've been invited to the Highland Country Club."

Olivia's eyebrows rose off her forehead. "Really? That's quite exclusive."

"I have a client who is a member. We're going as her guests."

"I can't imagine Austin at the Highland Country Club," Hannah said with a smile. "Some of those people are so stuffy! I'd love to see the look on their faces when he walks in wearing his cowboy hat."

That's exactly what Dana was afraid of. If only Austin would consider leaving the boots and hat at home and wearing a nice suit and tie, instead. Clothes that didn't scream cowboy. But how could she ask him to do that without offending him? There had to be a way.

And she had only twenty-four hours to find it.

CHAPTER EIGHT

"TELL ME HOW YOUR JOB works again," Austin said as they rode in the back seat of a Lincoln Town Car. "You agree to recommend a certain business to your clients, and in return they give you a bunch of free stuff?"

"No business is guaranteed a recommendation," Dana explained. "The vendor has to meet the high quality of service I want for my clients. That's why I need to try a business out first. Most owners understand this and know that providing a complimentary service now might pay off big for them later."

"So that's how we scored a free ride to this country club shindig," he concluded. "And why I'm trapped in this tuxedo tonight. To see if both the limo and the tux meet with your approval?"

Dana glanced over at her date for the evening. Austin looked absolutely devastating in the black Perry Ellis tuxedo. It defined the wide breadth of his shoulders and gave him an air of sophistication that made her much more optimistic about their evening at the Highland Country Club.

He definitely met with her approval.

"That tuxedo looks like it was made for you," she told him.

"Maybe so, but the shoes pinch," he complained, then reached up to adjust the black bow tie.

"That's just because you're used to wearing cow-boy boots. Consider this an adventure."

"Or a fairy tale." His gaze lingered on her. "You look like Cinderella dressed up for the ball."

Dana had spent hours preparing for this evening. She'd had her hair and nails done, courtesy of Paolo. Then she'd found the perfect sapphire-blue gown in Marco's studio. He'd given her permission to borrow any of his designs. He considered it good advertising.

"Is it too much?" she asked, suddenly worried as she looked down at the sleeveless dress studded with tiny crystal beads. The top of the heart-shaped bodice hugged her figure, while the full skirt flared at her hips and swirled around her ankles. "Do I look ridiculous?"

"You look incredible."

She knew he wasn't just saying what she wanted to hear. Austin didn't believe in empty flattery. He always told the plain and simple truth. It was one of the things she admired about him.

It was also one of the reasons she had worried about bringing him to the country club this evening. Dana had come to appreciate Austin's blunt honesty, but some of the more affluent people they met tonight, who were used to a certain amount of deference, might take offense.

Dana had worked for years to be welcome at a place like the Highland Country Club. The networking opportunities alone could prove a tremendous asset to her business. She knew people like the Van Hoeks and the Oxleys judged others by the company they kept. So she just hoped everyone liked Austin as much as she did.

"By the way, it's not a shindig," she told him as the car turned into the crowded parking lot of the country club. "It's a Valentine's Day Ball."

Another thought occurred to her. "Do you know how to dance?"

"Sure." He grinned. "I'm downright famous for my Texas two-step."

She swallowed a sigh. "I doubt they'll be playing any Dixie Chicks tonight."

"Don't worry, Dana," he said as the chauffeur pulled up to the front entrance. "I'll try not to step on your toes—or anybody else's."

She grabbed her wrap, a diaphanous blue silk that did little to keep the cold night air off her bare shoulders. Then she waited for the chauffeur to open her door before she stepped out onto the walk.

"When would you like me to return?" the chauffeur asked, as Austin climbed out of the other side of the car.

If she was playing Cinderella, she might as well go all the way. "How about midnight?"

The chauffeur nodded. "Very good. Have a pleasant evening."

As the Town Car pulled away, Austin walked over to join her at the door. "How does the limousine service rate?"

"So far, so good. We'll see if he's back here by midnight, before I give my final approval."

Dana gave the doorman their names, and after checking his list, he let them inside. She walked slowly through the foyer, absorbing every detail. Crystal

chandeliers hung from the dome ceiling, reflecting off
the Italian marble floor. The place was even more lav-
ish than she had imagined.

A friend of Dana's from the trailer park had once
worked here as a waitress. She'd complained about the
patronizing attitude of some of the members, though
the generous tips had made it more tolerable.

That hadn't altered Dana's dream to become a member someday. To mingle among people with power and
wealth. A United States senator was a member here.
The mayor's family, too. Doctors, lawyers, city council
members. Everyone who mattered.

Now she was part of their circle. An invited guest
who would be welcome as an equal among them. It
was a heady feeling for a girl from the wrong side of
the tracks.

"Is this all there is?" Austin asked, looking around
the club.

"There are tennis courts out back," she explained.
"Along with a pool."

He shook his head in amazement. "Wow."

"Impressive, isn't it?"

"Actually, I was just wondering who would pay
thousands of dollars in membership fees just to belong
to a glorified restaurant."

"It's not the place they're paying for," she replied,
a little stung by his criticism. "It's the atmosphere.
The privilege of belonging here."

He looked at her. "But who decides who can belong?"

"There's a committee that vets all applicants.
They're very selective."

"Exactly who are they trying to keep out?"

Before she could answer, Alison approached them, wearing a striking red Dior gown and a welcoming smile.

"I'm so glad you two could make it," Alison exclaimed. "Most of the gang is already here. We saved a place for you at our table. Just follow me."

Dana had never been part of the old gang, but they still greeted her with effusive welcomes.

"Hey, everyone, this is Dana Ulrich and Austin Hawke," Alison announced. "Dana is my fabulous wedding planner and she actually graduated from Westwood High with our class."

Startled exclamations sounded around the table, though Dana noticed that most of the women looked more interested in Austin.

"Dana, I'm sure you remember Phoebe Mills, Chloe Vance and Nina Haverman."

She did remember them. They'd been the elite in high school, looking right through her whenever she passed them in the school hallways. Funny how that still bothered her a little after all these years.

Especially since she was sure they had no memory of her.

"Phoebe is an attorney with Randolph, Cullings and Wright," Alison continued as they all sat down. "Her fiancé, Darrin, couldn't make it this evening. He's on duty at Seattle Memorial Hospital."

"He's a cardiology resident there," Phoebe informed them. "So I'm going stag tonight with Nina and Chloe."

"I still say you should convince him to go into plastic surgery," Nina said. "Then he'd at least work decent hours."

"You just want a discount on liposuction," Chloe teased.

Nina laughed. "Speak for yourself."

Alison looked around the club. "Clark is here somewhere, too. I sent him after drinks ten minutes ago."

"The service gets worse every time I come here," Phoebe complained.

Nina nodded. "At least they hired a decent band this time."

Chloe turned to Dana. "So you're a wedding planner." Then recognition lit her eyes. "*Dana Ulrich.* Oh, aren't you the one they call the—"

"This is one of my favorite songs," Austin interjected. "Any of you ladies care to dance?"

"I will," Chloe volunteered, jumping to her feet.

Dana breathed a sigh of relief that the topic of the wedding jinx had been avoided—for now. She watched Austin escort Chloe onto the dance floor, where the woman snaked her arms around his neck and pressed her body flush against his.

She turned away, jealousy coiling deep inside her. It was ridiculous, of course, since she had no claim on the man. She just hated to see a shallow opportunist like Chloe Vance get her claws into him.

"How long have you been planning weddings?" Nina asked her.

"On and off for several years for clients of Marco Kahn," Dana replied.

Nina looked impressed. "The designer Marco Kahn?"

She nodded. "The one and only."

"Wow, he's fabulous."

"He had a full-time wedding planner on his staff, and when she retired, he suggested I take her place."

Dana didn't mention that she had no college degree to back her up. Her parents couldn't even afford to send her to the local university. She'd needed to get a job right out of high school just to help them pay the outstanding debts that had piled up during her father's long illness. So she'd started working for Marco as a receptionist—a minimum-wage job that barely paid the bills—then slowly worked her way up.

"But don't you have your own business?" Phoebe asked, looking slightly confused.

"Yes, I decided to strike out on my own after Marco moved to Europe."

"I'll bet you have some wonderful wedding stories," Alison said. "Horror stories, too, I imagine."

"A few," she replied, glancing back at the dance floor. She couldn't tell if Austin was enjoying himself, though it was obvious by the way many of the female club members, including Chloe, were ogling him that they were enjoying *him.*

"Oh, do tell," Nina implored. "This ball is about to bore me to tears."

Dana searched her memory. "Well, I did have one bride who wanted to include eucalyptus in her bridal bouquet because she loved the fragrance. Unfortunately, she didn't know her groom was allergic to it. He broke out in hives from head to toe, right at the altar."

"Oh, no," Phoebe exclaimed with horrified laughter. "How awful!"

"The poor man tried to ride it out," Dana continued, "but after a while he couldn't take the itching anymore and literally started tearing off his clothes. The mother of the bride fainted and the bride herself began having hysterics and hitting him with her bouquet, which only made his hives worse.''

"What a nightmare,'' Alison said, as Austin and Chloe finally returned to the table and resumed their seats.

"Then what happened?'' Nina asked.

"The mother of the groom intervened,'' Dana said. "She informed the bride about the allergy, threw away the bouquet, then turned to the two hundred guests and asked if anyone had any Benadryl.''

"Forget the Benadryl,'' Nina said. "I would have taken it as a sign that I was marrying the wrong man and walked out the door.''

"She wouldn't if she truly loved him,'' Alison argued. "I wouldn't let hives or anything else stand in the way of marrying the man of my dreams.''

"That's because you've become a hopeless romantic ever since Clark proposed to you,'' Chloe replied.

"Be quiet, you two,'' Phoebe ordered. "Let Dana finish the story.''

"Well, one of the guests did have an antihistamine, and after it kicked in, the groom put his clothes back on and they continued the ceremony.''

"And lived happily ever after?'' Austin asked.

She met his gaze. "Yes, they did. So far, anyway.''

Alison suppressed a shudder. "I hope nothing like that happens at my wedding.''

"I don't know,'' Chloe countered, a mischievous gleam in her eye. "I think I'd enjoy watching Clark tear off all his clothes.''

"Your wish is my command,'' Clark said, arriving

at the table with a tray of drinks. "Just let me put these glasses down first."

"Very funny," Alison said, making room for him beside her. "Look who showed up while you were gone."

Clark nodded pleasantly to Dana, then reached across the table to shake Austin's hand. "Nice to see you both again. Sorry I wasn't here earlier. There's been some sort of walkout by some of the waitstaff, and the line at the bar is a mile long."

"Austin and Dana need a drink," Alison said as Clark began passing the glasses around the table.

"I can get them," Austin said, rising. He turned to Dana. "What would you like?"

"Try an amaretto sour," Chloe suggested, lifting the straw out of her glass. "They're sinfully delicious."

"That sounds good," Dana told him. He nodded, then headed off toward the bar.

As soon as he left the table, the interrogation began.

"He's gorgeous," Nina said, watching Austin walk away. "Where did you find him?"

"He just showed up on my doorstep one day," Dana replied honestly.

"I should be so lucky," Chloe said with a sidelong glance at her friends. "Please tell me he has a brother."

"He does," Dana replied, "but Jack's engaged."

Phoebe leaned back in her chair, sipping her drink. "So, what does Austin do for a living?"

"He's a cowboy," Alison announced, with the same awe in her voice as if he were an astronaut. "A *real* cowboy with a horse and everything."

Nina wrinkled her nose. "A cowboy?"

"He owns a ranch," Dana clarified. "In Texas."

"Well, he certainly cleans up nice for a cowboy," Phoebe observed. "The only cowboy I've ever seen was J.R. from reruns of that old television show. What was the name again…?"

"Dallas," Alison informed her. "But J.R. was more of an oilman than a cowboy. Even with the hat."

"Does Austin have any oil wells on his ranch?" Nina asked, arching a speculative brow.

"I really don't know," Dana hedged, though she doubted he'd need a bank loan if he did. "I suppose it's possible. It sounds as if his ranch covers quite a bit of land."

Chloe smiled. "Judging by that tuxedo he's got on, I'd say it's more than possible. He's probably as rich as J.R."

"But with much better taste in clothes," Nina said, laughing.

Chloe joined in. "Rich *and* sexy. My favorite combination."

Dana laughed along with the rest of them, then froze when she felt a broad hand on her shoulder. She craned her neck to see Austin standing behind her.

He set their drinks on the table, then said, "Let's dance."

Without waiting for her to reply, he headed for the dance floor, leaving Dana no choice but to follow him.

He turned and pulled her into his arms, his gray eyes as hard as flint. "What the hell was that all about?"

"What?" she asked, feeling the tension in his body.

"That crap you were telling those women about me. I'm no rich Texas land baron."

"I didn't tell them that. They just…assumed."

His eyes narrowed. "And you didn't say anything to correct that assumption?"

She'd never seen him this angry before. "You do own a ranch."

"I own half a ranch, which consists of a broken-down barn, a ninety-year-old house and a thousand acres of dry pasture ground. The only way I'll own the other half is if I make sure you don't screw up Jack and Hannah's wedding."

She stumbled at his words, and he drew his arms more tightly around her. "What are you talking about?"

"Forget it."

"No." She looked up into his eyes. "Tell me."

A muscle flexed in his jaw. "I came to Seattle to tell Jack that my father left him half of the Hawke Ranch in his will. Jack agreed to sell it to me, even though he could get more money a lot faster if he sold it to someone else."

"Why would he want to sell to someone else?"

"Simply because I'm almost broke, Dana. Any money I have saved up is going back into the ranch. The rest will have to come from a bank loan, if I qualify. There's no oil on my land. And I'm no cattle baron. Not yet, anyway. Not by a long shot."

"I still don't understand what this has to do with helping me plan their wedding."

"Because that was a stipulation Hannah put on the sale. I know it was just a ploy to get me to stay around Seattle for a while so Jack and I could get to know each other again. But I agreed to it, anyway."

Her throat was so tight that it was hard to speak.

"So you're with me right now because it's just part of a sales contract?"

"I'm with you because I want to be with you," Austin snapped. "Which is more than I can say for you. I'm just a prop for you, aren't I? Someone you can dress up in this monkey suit to fool all your friends. Hell, they're not even your friends. Why does their opinion matter so damn much to you?"

Tears stung her eyes, but she blinked them back. She refused to cry over a simple question. "I'm sorry. I didn't mean to embarrass you."

"Don't you get it?" Austin said, stepping away from her. "I'm not embarrassed. I'm not ashamed of who I am, either. Though you seem to be."

Then he turned around and walked away.

Dana started after him, but Clark intercepted her.

"May I have this dance?" he asked politely.

"This really isn't a good time," Dana replied, searching over his shoulder for Austin. But she couldn't see him anywhere in the crowd.

"Please," Clark said, holding out his arms.

She saw Alison watching them and knew it wouldn't make good business sense to refuse him. Besides, maybe she should give Austin some time to cool off. He'd been so angry with her—and for good reason.

She just hoped he'd come back.

"Fine," she said, tensing a little as Clark placed one hand at her waist.

"I know this is awkward as hell," he said, keeping a decent distance between them. "I meant to do this in your kitchen the other day, but it really wasn't the right time or place."

"Do what?" she asked warily.

"I want to apologize, Dana, for what happened between us back in high school. I take full responsibility."

She looked up at him in surprise. "Clark Oxley apologize? Did hell just freeze over?"

"I suppose I deserve that," he said wryly. "I was an eighteen-year-old jerk with an overinflated ego. I know that now."

"What you did was illegal. It's called sexual harassment."

He looked taken aback by her bluntness. "To be honest, I don't remember too many details from my senior year. I'd been drinking quite a lot."

She recalled the odor of gin on his breath the night of their supposed date. It had made her gag when he tried to kiss her.

"I know that's not an excuse," he conceded, "but it didn't take me long to realize that alcohol has a negative effect on me."

"I'd say that's an understatement."

He nodded. "That's exactly the reason I quit drinking."

Dana had noticed the soda in his glass tonight. Maybe he was speaking the truth. "Why are you telling me all of this now?"

"Hoping for absolution, I guess," he said with a shrug. "And to thank you for not letting the past interfere with the future."

"So you've never told Alison?"

He shook his head. "I didn't realize who you were until after she'd hired you. Since you didn't seem to have a problem with it, I didn't see the point."

Dana didn't know what to say to that. She did have

a problem with it, but she'd been too desperate at the time to turn down the job.

But there was still one question she had to ask. "Do you really love her?"

Despite her determination to see this wedding through to the end, her conscience had pricked her on more than one occasion. Austin had been so certain that she should tell Alison everything.

"I love her more than anything," Clark said softly. "She and I...we're like one person. She's my heart. My soul. My conscience."

"Before tonight, I didn't think you had a conscience."

"I don't blame you, especially after the way I treated you. I just want you to know that I'm sorry for any pain I caused you. I don't expect you to forgive me, but I hope you know how deeply I regret it."

The music finally came to an end, and Dana stepped away from him. "Thank you for telling me."

"Thank you for the dance," he said.

They returned to the table, but Austin still wasn't there. She picked up the amaretto sour in front of her and took a long sip, feeling slightly off-kilter. Clark's apology had been as unexpected as Austin's outburst of temper.

How could she convince Austin that he didn't embarrass her? That making a good impression was simply part of her business. A very vital part.

The rest of the evening passed in a blur. Austin eventually came back to the table, but he barely said a word to her or anyone else. Dana tried to enjoy herself, but it didn't take her long to realize that Austin was right. These people weren't her friends. She found herself slightly irritated with Chloe and Nina's inane chatter. And Phoebe spent most of the time on her cell phone talking to her busy doctor fiancé, while Clark and Alison danced the night away.

Midnight finally arrived, and she was more than ready for her sullen prince to turn back into a cowboy. They walked outside, but the Town Car hadn't arrived yet.

She looked up at Austin as they stood under the canopy, though it was hard to see his expression in the shadows. "Everyone liked you."

"And that makes you happy?"

She shook her head. "That's not what I meant. You seem to fit in so easily. I've never been able to do that. I always worry about doing or saying just the right thing. Knowing the right clothes to wear."

"Have you ever tried just being yourself?"

"I tried it a long time ago," she said. "But I found out it wasn't good enough."

He sighed. "Damn it, Dana, why does it matter so much what those people in there think about you?"

The breeze picked up as the car finally arrived. "Do you really want to know?" she asked.

"Yes," he replied as the chauffeur stepped out to open the back door for them.

"Then, I'll show you."

CHAPTER NINE

DANA DIRECTED THE CHAUFFEUR to a part of Seattle that Austin had never been to before. It was a long drive from the Highland Country Club, and the streets grew seedier with each passing block.

"Where are we going?" he asked at last.

She activated the privacy screen, sealing off the driver from their conversation. "My old neighborhood."

He knew she wanted to prove something to him, but Austin didn't realize until the car pulled up along a curb and came to a stop how different two parts of the same city could be. He looked out the window to see a trailer-park community illuminated under the street lights. There were trailers of all shapes and sizes inside, although most of them seemed to be in a state of disrepair. Broken screens. Peeling paint. All bordered by a rusty chain-link fence with several gaping holes. Hopelessness seemed to permeate the air.

"You wanted to know why impressing people at the country club was important to me," she said softly into the darkness. "This is why. Because I could end up right back here, living in the first trailer on the left."

His gaze moved in that direction and he saw a pale pink double-wide trailer hunkered on a small plot of withered grass. "That's where you grew up?"

"Yes," she replied. "And I used to dream about escaping from this place on a daily basis."

"But you did escape," he said, turning to face her. "You've got your business, your apartment."

She shook her head. "You've got it wrong, Austin. My life is an illusion. I'm barely making ends meet."

He opened his mouth to contradict her, then realized he'd only seen what she'd wanted him to see. But when he looked past all the background props that had made him stereotype her as a spoiled city girl the first time they'd met, the clues seemed obvious.

Dana was living rent-free in that fancy apartment, house-sitting for her former employer until his lease was up next month. Her cupboards were almost empty. Her refrigerator was practically bare except for the groceries he'd supplied. Her day-to-day existence consisted of goods and services supplied by vendors hoping for her business. That's how she survived. She was too thin because she didn't have enough food to eat, not because of some fad diet.

He felt like an idiot for not seeing the truth sooner.

"That's why working the Van Hoek wedding is so important to me," she continued, her voice tight. "Why I have to move in the right social circles if I want to be a success."

"There will be other weddings…" he began.

But she shook her head. "This is my last chance, Austin. My business will be finished if this wedding falls through."

He knew in his gut that she'd do anything to prevent that from happening. His Dana was a fighter, something he'd had to become himself to survive life with his father. A life he wouldn't want to go back to, either. That's what Dana was facing now.

"Do your parents still live there?" he asked.

"My mother does, though I don't see her nearly as often as I'd like. My father passed away three years ago. He never escaped."

Austin heard the pain in her voice and wished like hell he could take back some of the harsh words he'd said to her tonight. He'd been looking at her life from his vantage point, not hers.

He could see now that the view was very different.

LATER THAT NIGHT, Austin lay stretched out in his bedroll on the apartment floor, his hands folded behind his head. A small fire burned in the hearth, casting shadows that danced on the ceiling.

He'd seen the real Dana tonight and finally understood what drove her. But now he'd begun to wonder what it would take for Dana to see him—the real him, not the man she wanted him to be. He'd learned the hard way that he couldn't live his life to please other people.

His father had never thought he and Jack were good enough. They'd always been too slow. Too dumb. Too lazy. It had become Lincoln Hawke's mantra. At one time, Austin had turned himself inside out to try to become the son that Linc had wanted him to be.

Jack had gone the opposite direction, raising hell on a daily basis. Soon Austin had seen that it didn't make any difference. No matter what either one of his sons did, Linc viewed them both as a troublesome burden that he didn't want to bear alone.

That's when Austin had given up trying to be perfect. He'd become just as wild as Jack, determined to live life to the fullest, no matter what the consequences.

He shifted in the bedroll, remembering the pain of some of those consequences. He'd gotten into a lot of bar fights, broken too many hearts to count, and had his own heart broken, as well. But he'd never wanted to be somebody else—somebody better.

Until tonight.

Austin turned around and punched his feather pillow, wishing it were Clark Oxley's face. It felt so good, he did it a second time. He didn't like that rich city boy and he sure as hell didn't trust him, even if Dana did want to believe the man had changed for the better.

Hell, why should Austin even care? He'd never fit into that kind of crowd, anyway. He wasn't sure he wanted to fit in. He might not have money or stock options or a country club membership, but he did have his pride.

A short time later, Dana whispered in the dark, "Are you still awake?"

He rolled onto his back to see her kneeling beside him. She wore a long, black-satin nightgown with lace at the bodice and hem. Her eyes gleamed silver in the firelight, her short dark hair a silken frame around her beautiful face. If only she could see herself as he saw her.

"I can't sleep," she confessed.

He sat up, the blanket falling to his waist. "Neither can I."

Her gaze darted to his bare chest, then met his eyes

once more. "I don't blame you for being angry with me tonight."

"I'm not angry anymore." Austin hesitated, not sure he should go on. He knew that the way Dana lived her life was none of his business, but he couldn't seem to stop himself. "I just wish those people didn't matter so much to you. Life's too short to care what anybody else thinks."

"It's not that easy for me," she replied. "I have dreams, Austin. Huge goals that I set for myself years ago. To accomplish them, I need those people in that club tonight. It's vital to my career. It's vital to me."

"I know all about dreams," he said huskily. "I've lived my entire life with the dream of someday taking over the Hawke Ranch. Sometimes it was the only thing that kept me going—like after my mother died."

She reached out to touch his arm, her gentle fingertips blazing a sensual trail as they slid up to his bare shoulder. "Then, maybe we're more alike than we think. I just hope we can still be…friends."

"Is that what we are?" he asked huskily, reaching out to caress her cheek. "Just friends?"

Her breathing quickened, but she didn't move as he slid one knuckle along the creamy smoothness of her jawline, then down the length of her neck.

"You tell me," she whispered, her lips parting.

"A friend wouldn't want to do this," he said, leaning forward to kiss the soft pulse at the base of her throat, before skimming his lips up her neck.

"Or this," he breathed, brushing a light kiss over the fullness of her mouth. She moaned softly when he pulled away, but Austin wasn't finished. He wanted her to know exactly how he felt about her.

"I like every part of you," he said, his lips moving over her face. "Your nose. Your chin. Your gorgeous eyes."

Regret shimmered in those eyes as she looked up at him. "Austin, I'm sorry I misled those people about you at the country club tonight. I know that you were the best man there, with or without the tuxedo."

"Then, make it up to me," he said hoarsely.

Regret turned to uncertainty. "What do you have in mind?"

"A dance." He held out his hand. "Only, this time I promise not to walk away."

She hesitated only a moment before placing her hand in his. Austin's heart galloped in his chest as he rose, tugging up the elastic waistband of his sweatpants.

She reached over to switch on the stereo, then fiddled with the dial before finding a country music station playing the oldies. When Patsy Cline began singing "Crazy," Dana stepped into his arms.

Austin's hands cradled her hips as they began swaying together to the music, their eyes on each other. Her silky softness inflamed him until the fire in the hearth was nothing compared with the blaze burning inside him.

"I want to be more than friends," he said, gazing at her.

"Me, too," she breathed, pulling him closer before she leaned up for a kiss. A kiss that started out with as much yearning as the song on the stereo. A kiss that filled some deep, empty place inside of him.

Her hands splayed over his bare chest, his muscles contracting beneath her featherlight touch. When a tiny moan emanated from deep in her throat, Austin lost his last shred of restraint.

His tongue met hers as the kiss became something more. Something inevitable. She arched toward him until her breast met his palm. He cradled the fullness of it in his hand, his thumb teasing her nipple through the satin nightgown.

She moaned again at the sensation, her hands now feverishly touching him everywhere. He wanted to go slowly, to savor every moment, every precious inch of her. But his body pounded with need until he finally swept her up into his arms and carried her to the bedroom.

He laid her on the mattress, then kissed her again as her nightgown slipped off one shoulder. For just a moment, he drank in the sight of her there, sprawled against the pillows, her pink lips parted with anticipation.

Austin couldn't think straight when she looked at him like that. Then she sat up and pulled the nightgown over her head, revealing full breasts with taut nipples that he ached to taste.

He couldn't remember wanting a woman this much, and that scared him a little. But the only thing that scared him more was letting her go. He shoved the unsettling thought aside as he lay down beside her, one hand sliding over her bare hip.

Then he rolled on top of her, sinking into her soft, inviting body. She wrapped her arms around his neck, flexing her hips against him, and Austin groaned at the sensation as his desire for her spun out of control.

Their passion for each other overcame everything else. He barely remembered to roll on a condom, almost coming undone when she helped him, her nimble fingers inflaming him even more. Then he was on top of her again, inside of her, rocking into her with a desperation born of need.

She matched his rhythm until it reached a shattering crescendo that left them both gasping for breath.

Austin held on to her tightly, their hearts beating as one.

They lay for a time in each other's arms, spent and sated. Then Dana breathed a deep sigh of contentment as she drifted off to sleep. "My cowboy."

Austin wasn't sure if she knew what she was saying, but it didn't matter. It was too close to the truth. If he wasn't very careful he would be hers—body and soul.

THEY MADE LOVE AGAIN when the sun came up.

Dana had thought last night was a dream, until she woke up to find Austin naked in her bed. Naked and aroused. He loved her slowly, tenderly, as the first rays of sunlight seeped through the bedroom window.

Then he made her breakfast.

"I could get used to this," Dana said, sitting up in bed so Austin could set the tray in front of her.

"See, there are advantages to waking up with the sun." He leaned over to kiss her, then plucked a strip of crispy bacon from her plate. "Even for a city girl like yourself."

She looked up at him, wondering if last night had changed anything between them. They still had different goals. Different dreams. They were perfect for each other in bed, but out of bed seemed to be another story.

"So what happens now?"

Austin headed for the door. "Now I'm going to hop

in the shower. You're welcome to join me when you're through with breakfast.''

That wasn't what she'd meant, and something told her Austin knew it. For a man who valued honesty, he didn't seem to want to face the problem before them. Last night had been wonderful, but how could it possibly last?

Then Dana realized she might be reading too much into it. Austin had made love to her, but she didn't have any reason to believe he wanted something more. On the contrary, he'd made it very clear last night that his future was in Texas. Just as hers was in Seattle.

Later that day, they drove to the Harbor Club on Second and Columbia to make the preliminary arrangements for holding Hannah and Jack's wedding there. They met Hannah's father, Kenneth Richards, outside the manager's office. Tall and fit, with dark brown hair and eyes, he looked young for his fifty-nine years.

Dana introduced herself, then motioned to Austin. ''I don't believe you've met Jack's brother. This is Austin Hawke.''

Kenneth shook their hands. ''It's a pleasure to meet you both.'' He glanced at his watch. ''Looks like my little girl is running late.''

''It sounds like she's pretty busy these days,'' Austin said.

Kenneth nodded, pride shining in his eyes. ''She's doing well for herself. Handling a new business. Planning a wedding. Giving me a grandson like Adam. I couldn't be happier about it.''

Dana and Austin exchanged glances, both wondering if Kenneth knew his daughter was expecting another baby. Austin had told Dana about Hannah's pregnancy when she'd lain in his arms last night. He'd also shared enough about his life and his family for her to see how those experiences had forged the man he was today. A man who was both strong and sensitive. Caring and confident.

A man she found herself more drawn to than ever after last night.

"Would you like a tour of the club?" Kenneth offered, breaking her reverie. "We can discuss specific details about the wedding and reception when Hannah arrives."

"I'd like that," she replied, glancing up at Austin. He was watching her, his eyes hooded. Dana wished she knew what he was thinking at this moment, but she didn't know him quite well enough to read his mind. Or his heart.

Kenneth showed them around the club, a place he obviously knew well. She understood why when they passed by the trophy case and she saw his name inscribed on several of the sailing trophies inside.

"You won all of these?" Dana asked, stopping in front of the display for a closer look.

Kenneth moved up beside her. "I've competed in quite a few sailing races over the years, though with different crews." He nodded toward the slightly tarnished gold cup on the top shelf of the case. "That was my first win, almost twenty-five years ago."

She took a closer look and saw two other names inscribed beside his. Louis Kinard and Jonathan Webber—his old friends and business partners, according to what Debbie North had told her.

"Those were good times," Kenneth mused, his

voice more subdued now. "You don't realize how much people mean to you until they're gone."

She thought of her Gram, and her throat grew tight. Then she looked up at Austin and remembered that he'd be going away after Jack and Hannah's wedding. The thought of losing him so soon created an ache deep inside her.

Dana shook it off, telling herself not to worry about the future. She had enough problems to deal with in the present. Like making sure both the Van Hoek wedding and Hannah's wedding ran as smoothly as possible.

"There's my girl," Kenneth announced, looking toward the door.

"Sorry I'm late," Hannah said, slightly breathless as she walked up to them. "What did I miss?"

"I just gave them the grand tour of the place," Kenneth replied, giving her a warm hug.

She kissed his weathered cheek, then turned to Dana. "Do you think this place will work for the wedding?"

"I think it will be perfect. We can use the north room for the ceremony, then open up the doors that lead to the dining room for the reception."

Hannah looked at Austin. "How about Jack? Do you think he'll like it?"

"He'll want whatever makes you happy," Austin replied. "The view itself is great." He nodded toward the wall of windows in front of them, which offered a spectacular prospect of Mount Rainier, Elliott Bay and the Olympic Mountains.

"It almost makes me wish I was out on the water right now," Hannah said with a wistful sigh.

"How about lunch with your old dad, instead?"

Kenneth offered, draping his arm around her shoulders. "We can talk about sailing all you like. You know I never get tired of the subject."

Hannah smiled. "Lunch sounds wonderful."

"Okay, you stay right here while I go reserve us a table." He looked up at Austin and Dana. "Would you two like to join us?"

"Thank you," Dana said, "but we really have to be going soon."

Kenneth nodded, then hurried away.

Hannah turned back to them with a small smile. "In case you hadn't noticed, my father loves sailing."

"That reminds me of something else I wanted to ask you," Dana said. "What do you think about making sailboat rides available to the guests at your reception?"

"That's a great idea," Hannah exclaimed. "It should be warm enough in April."

"It will be unique," Dana told her. "And definitely give a nautical flavor to the wedding."

"Then, let's do it," Hannah affirmed.

"On one condition," Austin said. "Your future brother-in-law does not have to go sailing."

"Oh, Austin, you should try it," Hannah insisted. "It's wonderful."

"My stomach and I prefer to stay on solid ground, thank you very much."

"Spoken like a true cowboy," Hannah mused. "What are we going to do with him, Dana?"

That same question had been gnawing at her ever since she'd awoken this morning in his arms. "I honestly don't know."

HANNAH LEANED AGAINST the rail on the balcony, her hair flying in the breeze as she looked out over Puget

Sound. They'd finished lunch and walked out onto the empty balcony after dessert. It was too cold for most people, but Kenneth and Hannah had never let that stop them before.

"Are you warm enough?" Kenneth stood beside her, doing his best to block the wind.

"I'm fine, Dad," she replied. But in truth, she hadn't been fine since learning that her blood type didn't square up with those of her parents.

Jack thought she should drop the issue. Even on the unlikely chance that it were true, the people who'd raised her *were* her real parents, he'd said, not the sperm and egg donor.

Hannah couldn't blame him for feeling that way. Jack had lost his father shortly after he was born and his mother when he was a teenager. On top of that, he'd been saddled with an emotionally abusive step-father. From his vantage point, she had two loving parents, so why go looking for trouble?

But trouble had found her.

Hannah wished she could just put it behind her. Pretend that everything was perfect in her world. But that would be living a lie.

The question was, had she been living a lie her entire life?

During lunch, Hannah hadn't been able to bring up the subject of the blood tests. Once her father got started talking about sailing, he didn't stop. But now the time had finally come.

"I have some good news, Dad," she said, moving close enough to him so that he could hear her over the wind.

Kenneth smiled at her. "More good news? You've already given me a grandson and a future son-in-law. I don't know if I can stand any more."

"Well, I hope you can, because Jack and I are expecting another baby."

"Ah, honey," he said, wrapping her in his arms. "That's terrific."

Hannah inhaled the spicy scent of his aftershave, so familiar to her after all these years. She remembered how her mother used to complain before their divorce that Kenneth never changed. He always used the same aftershave, wore the same silly sailing hat, drove the same make of car, year after year.

But his stability was one of the things Hannah loved about him. She could always count on her father to be there for her. To protect her from the storms that life tossed her way.

"There's something else, Dad."

The tone of her voice made him pull away, his brow wrinkled. "What is it, honey?"

She swallowed. "When I was at the obstetrician's office, the nurse discovered that there's some kind of discrepancy with our blood types."

Worry clouded his eyes. "You mean there's something wrong with the baby?"

"No," she assured him, regretting that it had come out that way. This was difficult enough without confusing the issue. "It has nothing to do with the baby. I'm blood type A positive. But apparently, that can't be possible with parents who both have negative blood types, like you and Mom."

He squinted into the sun. "What's that supposed to mean?"

She took a deep breath. "It means that one of you can't be my biological parent."

He stared at her for a moment, then clenched his jaw. "That's impossible."

"There's a chance there was a mistake in one of the blood tests we all took back when you had your car accident," she conceded, "but—"

"No buts about it," he said. "It's a mistake, plain and simple. I'm your father, Hannah. I'll always be your father, no matter what some damn, incompetent lab test has to say about it."

"I know that, Dad," she said, her throat aching. She could tell by his expression that he wasn't willing to even consider another possibility.

"I can't believe that nurse would upset you with something like this," he said, his tone gentler now. "Honey, this is nothing for you to worry about. All you have to do is concentrate on having a healthy baby."

"I know." Hannah turned and looked out over the water. Either the blood test was wrong, or her mother and father were lying. She wanted so badly to blame this on a medical mistake, but when she'd asked the doctor later if the tests could be wrong, she'd made it clear that was very unlikely.

She'd find no answers today. Her parents might be divorced, but they were unified in their insistence that she was their child.

Maybe Jack was right. Maybe that was enough.

LATE THAT NIGHT, Kenneth Richards sat on the balcony of his high-rise condo. It afforded a fabulous view of downtown Seattle and the Space Needle, but he was too shell-shocked at the moment to notice. Wrapped in blankets to keep out the cold, he sat staring out over the city with a bottle of scotch in his hand.

He took another long drag on the bottle, still waiting for the numbness to set in. He'd barely made it back from the club in one piece, so distracted that he'd run a stop light at a major intersection.

There's some kind of discrepancy with our blood types.

"Damn you, Olivia," he muttered, draining the bottle. He tossed it away from him, hearing the satisfying smash of glass against the deck.

Kenneth leaned his head against the chair and closed his eyes, forgetting about the broken glass. He'd clean up the mess tomorrow. Hell, he was used to cleaning up messes. The disaster at Eagle Aerotech. His trainwreck of a marriage. And now this.

One of you can't be my biological parent.

His alcohol-soaked mind drifted back to those early years with Olivia Brawney Richards. The moment he'd laid eyes on her, Kenneth had known she was the perfect woman for him. Polished, educated and ambitious. After a short courtship, they'd married and bought a house on Forrester Square South, close to the Kinards and Webbers.

Naturally, the next step was having a baby. They'd wanted one so badly, but the endless months of trying without success had eventually put a strain on their marriage. Olivia thought her husband blamed her and she grew resentful. She began going out more and more without him, finding new friends of her own. Like that French playboy, Paul Marchand.

But the fault didn't lie with his wife. Kenneth had gone to have himself secretly checked out by a doctor, only to find his worst fear confirmed—he was sterile.

The doctor had told him it was probably the result of a childhood bout with scarlet fever. But the reason didn't matter to Kenneth. He was sterile. Half a man. A dismal failure as a husband.

He'd never told Olivia about that sperm test. Maybe that had been unfair to her, but Kenneth just couldn't make himself admit it aloud. Hell, he'd barely been able to admit it to himself.

When he and Olivia grew even further apart, he'd blamed himself. Kenneth suspected his wife was having affairs, but he was still shocked when she'd turned up pregnant. He tried to tell himself that he was the father. That some miracle had occurred. But deep inside, he'd always known the truth.

He wasn't Hannah's father.

A wrenching sob choked him, but he swallowed hard to keep from losing control. He might not be Hannah's biological father, but she was still his daughter in every way that really mattered.

When Hannah was younger, he used to wonder if Paul Marchand was her biological father. Hannah had blue eyes and light hair like the man. And he knew Olivia had spent an inordinate amount of time with the charming Marchand.

Kenneth released a deep sigh, pushing those thoughts back into the attic of his memory. What did it really matter now who his ex-wife had slept with?

As he drew the blankets more tightly around him, he felt the blessed numbness overtake him, the vodka finally kicking in. He stood up to go inside, still sober enough to know he could pass out and freeze to death in the cold. But as he stumbled through the door, the warmth of the house enveloped him and he began to feel sick to his stomach.

Hannah suspected. His sweet Hannah suspected.

Sagging onto the nearest chair, he buried his head in his hands, unable to stop the hot tears flowing through his fingers. After all these years, the awful truth threatened to take his little girl away from him.

"Never," he cried out, raising his head and sucking in a deep, determined breath. "Hannah will never find out the truth!"

Kenneth didn't care what he had to do to stop it. He'd go to his death before he'd lose his only child.

CHAPTER TEN

THE NEXT DAY, Dana walked among the potted plants and hanging baskets at the Gilded Rose flower shop. With the Van Hoek wedding less than a week away, they'd finally set up a time for Alison to make some last-minute changes to her floral arrangements. Alison hadn't arrived yet, so Dana used the opportunity to daydream about Austin.

The sweet fragrance of lavender lingered in the air, reminding her of her grandmother. Gram would have liked Austin, Dana thought to herself. Especially his no-nonsense approach to life. Her grandmother had never abided people who made excuses for themselves. And she had been one of the first people to encourage Dana to go after her dream of becoming a wedding planner.

Dana liked Austin, too. A lot. That was the problem. She was falling in love with a man who would be leaving for Texas in five short weeks. Part of her wanted to convince him to stay with her, but how could she ask him to give up the cowboy life and his ranch? There was nothing for him in Seattle except her, and she had no reason to believe that would be enough for him.

"Dana?"

She turned around to see Clark Oxley standing next to a potted tree. "What are you doing here?"

"Alison couldn't make it," Clark explained with an apologetic shrug. "So she asked me to meet you here."

She didn't like the idea of being alone with this man, even if he had mended his ways. "I can schedule another time...."

"That's not necessary." He pulled a piece of paper from his shirt pocket. "Alison sent along a list of different flowers she likes that won't give anybody hives. After that eucalyptus story you told at the country club, she called the entire wedding party to find out if they had any floral allergies."

"Oh, no," Dana said, feeling awful. "I didn't mean to scare her."

"She'll be all right," Clark assured her. "I think she's just got a case of pre-wedding jitters."

Dana looked up at him. "How about you?"

He smiled. "I can't wait to make Alison my wife. I'd elope with her today if she'd let me."

"I don't think that's going to happen." Dana began to relax a little. Clark really did seem different—less cocky than he'd been as a teenager. Maybe he truly had changed.

"Why don't we go over the changes on the list with the florist?" she suggested. "Then I'll get together with Alison tonight or tomorrow and finalize everything."

"My fiancée is already one step ahead of you," Clark said with a note of pride in his voice. "Alison wants you to meet her tomorrow afternoon at her office suite in the Palace Hotel. She mentioned one o'clock, but if that doesn't work she's willing to reschedule.''

"One o'clock should be fine. We need to get the final order in as soon as possible.''

"Great.'' He looked around the florist's shop. "Where do we start?''

She led him to a small round table in the corner. "The owner already gave me the portfolios of his wedding arrangements. We'll compare the ones we like to Alison's list of flowers and see what will work the best for your wedding.''

Clark pulled out a chair for Dana, then sat down across from her. "Whatever you say is okay by me. I'm certainly no expert on flowers.''

They flipped through the portfolios for an hour, Dana and the florist making suggestions and Clark offering an opinion or two. Dana was pleasantly surprised to find herself actually enjoying his company. Clark was a perfect gentleman and a devoted bridegroom.

It just reaffirmed for her that his apology the other night had been genuine. She'd heard alcohol could alter your personality. Austin had claimed it had happened to his own father. And the eighteen-year-old Clark *had* been drinking the night he'd tried to pin her down in his car.

She didn't want to make excuses for him, but Dana suddenly felt much better about her decision not to tell Alison what had happened ten years ago.

After they had gone through all the floral portfolios and made their decisions, Clark walked with her to the parking lot. He bid her goodbye at the curb, heading toward his silver Porsche at the far end of the lot.

She unlocked the driver's door of the Beast, then slid behind the steering wheel, tossing the portfolios she'd borrowed from the owner onto the seat beside her. Hannah and Jack were going to use the same flower shop for their wedding, and Dana had suggested they look over what was available before she placed an order.

She stuck the car key into the ignition, but when she tried to start it, the engine made a sickly whirring sound. Flipping the switch off, she pumped the gas pedal three times, then tried it again.

No luck.

On the third attempt, she saw the silver flash of Clark's Porsche in her rearview mirror. He parked behind her, then got out of his car, the engine still running.

Trapped. Despite her earlier ease with him, panic clawed at her throat. She looked frantically around the parking lot, but there were no other people around. For a moment, she debated whether to make a run for the florist shop, but Clark was already headed her way.

Dana jabbed the automatic lock button, so he couldn't open any of the car doors. Then she cracked open her window as he approached the driver's side.

"Looks like you've got a problem," he said.

It took her a moment to realize he was talking about her car. "My car's a little temperamental," she replied, trying to make light of it. "Sometimes it's a little slow getting started."

"Why don't you let me give it a try?" he said, pulling on the door handle. "Hey, it's locked."

Dana hesitated, then unlocked the door, telling herself she was overreacting. Clark had done nothing recently to warrant this irrational fear.

As he climbed into the driver's seat, she hastily slid over to the passenger side, remembering all too clearly what had happened the last time she'd been alone in an automobile with him.

But she was thankful when he seemed oblivious to her, concentrating on the sound of her car's engine. Still, she wrapped her hand around the passenger door handle, ready to flee if he made one aggressive move toward her.

"I'm going to take a peek under the hood," he said, pulling on a lever beneath the dash. The hood of the car popped up, and Clark got out and rounded the front fender.

Breathing a deep and somewhat embarrassed sigh of relief, Dana joined him there. "You really shouldn't go to all this trouble. I can call a tow truck...."

"It's no trouble," he assured her, his head bent under the hood. "Working on cars is one of my hobbies. And I think I see the problem."

Completely ignorant as to the inner workings of automobiles, she watched as he adjusted some cables.

"There," he said, pulling out a handkerchief to wipe the grease off his hands. "That should solve the problem—temporarily, anyway. One of the electrical wires is loose. Why don't you try starting it now?"

She did as he suggested, slipping into the driver's seat and turning the key in the ignition. The Beast roared to life.

Dana leaned her head out the window as he slammed the hood down. "It works!"

"Hey, don't sound so surprised," he said with a

smile. "I think I was a mechanic in a former life. It seems to come naturally to me."

She pointed to his chin. "You have some grease…"

He wiped it off with his handkerchief. "Good thing you warned me. Alison hates it when I play grease monkey."

Dana didn't know what else to say to him. "Well…thank you."

"No problem," he replied, heading back to his car. Then he turned around. "Hey, do you want me to follow you in case it gives you any more trouble?"

"No thanks," she replied. "I'm not going very far and I have my cell phone with me."

"Okay, I'll see you later, then." Clark climbed into his Porsche and sped away.

Dana headed out of the parking lot onto the street, turning in the direction of Forrester Square Day Care. Austin wouldn't be happy about the fact that she'd met with Clark alone this afternoon. In fact, she might be better off not telling him about it. She didn't want to waste the time they had left together arguing about Clark Oxley.

When she dropped off the florist's portfolios at the day-care office, Dana was disappointed to find Hannah wasn't there. She left a sticky note on top of the desk, informing Hannah that she'd telephone her later in the week to see what kind of bridal bouquet she'd selected.

But once Dana was back in her car, she found she wasn't going anywhere. The Beast refused to start again, the engine completely dead now. She called Austin on her cell phone, asking him to pick her up. Then she sat out in the parking lot for ten minutes, hoping the Beast would miraculously come back to life. But the cold air finally drove her inside the building.

Carmen greeted her with smile. "Back again so soon?"

"My car won't start. Do you mind if I wait in here until Austin arrives?"

"Not at all. I'd like to meet this boyfriend of yours."

Dana felt an overwhelming urge to confide in the woman, but before she could open her mouth, several of the children began clamoring for Carmen's attention.

"Would you care to help us put together a puzzle?" Carmen asked her.

Dana nodded, welcoming the opportunity to push aside her own troubles for a while. "I'd love to."

AUSTIN STRODE INTO Forrester Square Day Care, anxious to see Dana again. They'd only been apart a few hours, but it had seemed like forever to him. That was a bad sign. If he didn't get his head on straight he'd be blubbering love poems to her and talking about making babies.

Not a good plan. How could this relationship possibly go anywhere when her top priority was fitting into Seattle's high society? And his was obtaining a bank loan so he could turn the Hawke Ranch into a profitable enterprise once more.

A long-distance relationship would never work, and there didn't seem to be any other options. At least, none that Austin could see.

The hallway and office were both empty, so he stuck

his head inside the door of the first classroom he came upon.

One little girl jumped to her feet when she saw him and pointed at his hat. "It's a cowboy!"

All the children turned to stare at him, and that's when he saw Dana sitting at an undersize table in front of a puzzle.

"Yes, it is a cowboy," Dana confirmed, smiling at him as she rose. "He's even got a horse."

The children gasped in amazement.

"A real horse?" the same little girl asked. "Or a stick horse?"

"It's a real horse," he replied, walking into the classroom.

A middle-aged woman with snapping black eyes and a warm smile walked over to him. "You must be Jack's brother. I'm Carmen Perez, the head teacher here at Forrester Square Day Care."

Austin tipped his hat to her. "Ma'am."

"Hannah's told me all about you," Carmen said. "I think the children would be fascinated to hear about the life of a real cowboy. Do you have time to stay for a while?"

"That's up to Dana," he replied, looking to her for guidance.

"It's fine with me." She sat back down in a miniature chair. "I'd like to hear about the cowboy life, too."

Something about the way she said it made him look back at her. Was it possible she might consider coming to Texas? He quickly put that improbable thought out of his mind. *Wishful thinking, cowboy.*

Carmen herded the children into the center of the

room and instructed them to sit on the floor. "Now, everyone needs to open their ears and listen very carefully to Mr. Hawke. He's going to tell us all about cowboys."

Dana watched with amusement as Austin tipped up his hat, looking like a nervous giant among the small bodies gathered around him.

"Perhaps the children could begin by asking you questions," Carmen suggested, "and you can take it from there."

"All right." Austin turned to face his young audience. "Fire away."

"What's your horse's name?" piped one little boy with a face full of freckles.

"Her name is Princess."

"You have a girl horse?" asked another boy, wrinkling his nose in disgust.

"She's called a mare," Austin said, perching himself on the edge of the table. "Princess helps me round up the cattle at night so I can feed them, and she also helps me find the strays."

"What's a stray?" asked the same freckle-faced boy.

"It's a cow or a calf that wanders away from the rest of the herd and gets lost."

"It's scary to get lost," commented a boy beside him.

"It sure is," Austin agreed. "One time there was a calf that was lost for three days, and I finally found him in the bottom of a dry gully. But I didn't know how to get him out...."

Dana watched the children lean forward, hanging on Austin's every word as he told the story of the lost calf. As she listened, she could see him grow more comfortable. He was good with children and he obviously loved his work. It reinforced to her that being a cowboy was more than a job for Austin, it was a way of life.

Half an hour later, Carmen sent the children off for a snack with a teacher's aide. Then she turned to Austin. "The children just loved you! Thank you so much for telling us all those wonderful stories."

"It was my pleasure, ma'am."

She laughed. "I just adore that Texas accent. No wonder Dana can't resist you."

Austin's gaze leveled on Dana. "Is that what she told you?"

"Oh, she didn't have to say a word," Carmen replied. "I can see the way she looks at you. Three of my own sons all recently fell in love and got married, so I recognize that look when I see it."

Before Dana could speak up for herself, a loud commotion broke out at the front entrance of the building. Carmen ran out into the hallway, Austin and Dana at her heels.

"Where is she?" shouted a tall man, storming inside the building. His jacket was askew and his graying brown hair was slightly rumpled.

"Mr. Tidwell, please," Carmen entreated, "keep your voice down."

The man, who looked close to sixty, seemed unaware of the terrified children gathered in the doorways. His gaze narrowed on Carmen through his wire glasses. She stood her ground as he charged forward.

"I want to see my daughter right now!"

"Amy's not here, Mr. Tidwell. You're scaring the children, so I'm going to have to ask you to leave."

"I'm not going anywhere until I talk to Amy."

Dana saw Austin shift slightly, positioning himself to intervene if necessary.

The man before them did look slightly unbalanced. Thick veins bulged in his neck, and his face was red with rage.

Carmen lowered her voice. "Please don't make me call the police, Mr. Tidwell."

Tidwell. Amy Tidwell. That was the name of the young girl who had recently had a baby, Dana remembered. The one staying in Hannah's apartment.

"I should be the one calling the police," Tidwell shouted, his voice even louder now. "You've practically kidnapped my only daughter—conspiring to brainwash her against me."

"We've done no such thing," Carmen said firmly. "Amy is eighteen years old and much more mature than most girls her age."

"I don't care how old she is. I'm still her father and..." His voice trailed off as his face went from red to purple.

A strange, gurgling noise emanated from his throat as his knees buckled.

Austin reached out and caught his arm to keep him from hitting the floor.

"Oh, dear," Carmen gasped, her hand flying to her chest. "What's wrong with him?"

"I'm not sure." Austin laid the man gently on the floor. "But you'd better call an ambulance."

Carmen rushed to a telephone while Dana kneeled beside Austin. She watched him loosen the man's tie, then unbutton the collar of his shirt. Then he checked his pulse. Tidwell remained unconscious.

"Will he be all right?"

"He's still breathing." Austin rolled up his brown leather coat into a makeshift pillow and used it to elevate the man's feet.

Carmen walked back over to them, her face wrenched with concern. "The ambulance is on its way and I called Amy. She'll meet me at the hospital. I told her she could bring the baby here to the nursery, but she had a friend visiting when I called and the girl offered to watch Leanne."

Austin rose. "Do you want us to give you a ride to the hospital?"

"Would you mind?" Carmen asked. "I'm in no condition to get behind a steering wheel at the moment, but I want to be at the hospital to support Amy."

"We'll be glad to do it," Dana said, as the shriek of a siren sounded on the street outside.

Carmen left briefly to inform the other teachers about what was happening and to ask one of them to fill in for her. Dana and Austin stayed by Russ Tidwell's side. His color had improved slightly, but he still looked very ill.

The ambulance crew rushed inside and took over, quickly assessing the situation, then hoisting Tidwell onto a portable gurney.

By the time the ambulance left, Carmen was ready to leave with them.

"I just got hold of Hannah," she said as they walked to the truck. "She's on her way to the hospital, too. She and Amy are very close."

Dana sat in the middle of the pickup cab, with Austin and Carmen on either side of her. Despite the busy rush-hour traffic, Austin made good time on the road.

"I've never seen Mr. Tidwell like that before," Carmen mused, shaking her head. "So full of anger."

Dana had never seen anyone so enraged. "He looked out of control."

The older woman nodded. "I think that's exactly the problem. He had such high expectations for Amy, and when she became pregnant...well, that was something he couldn't control."

"Is he married?" Austin asked.

Carmen shook her head. "His wife died when Amy was very young, so he raised her as a single father. He did a wonderful job, too. She's a delightful girl. I just wish he could see that."

They arrived at the hospital and met Amy in the visitors' area of the emergency room. The girl immediately fell sobbing into Carmen's outstretched arms.

Austin and Dana moved to the corner of the waiting room to give them some privacy.

"Poor kid," Austin said, his deep voice hushed.

Dana watched the girl until too many memories from her own past bubbled up inside her and she had to turn away. "I hope her father's all right."

"It will be tough on her if he doesn't make it," Austin observed. "They need a chance to patch things up."

"You sound like you speak from experience."

Austin shrugged. "I didn't get a chance to make peace with my father before he died. It's something I regret."

"You loved him," Dana said simply.

Austin cleared his throat. "Yeah, despite everything, I guess I did. I try to remember him the way he was before my mom died. Before he turned to a bottle for comfort instead of to his sons.''

She laid a hand on his arm, wishing she could erase the pain she glimpsed in his eyes. Austin wasn't a man to show his emotions, but she sensed they ran deep. Once again, she was struck by his empathy for other people, and realized that he would have made a good doctor if he had chosen that path. A path that might have led to a future for them.

They sat down on the orange vinyl chairs, sensing a long wait before they would receive any news on the condition of Russ Tidwell.

''I'm so glad you knew what to do for Mr. Tidwell,'' Dana said after several moments of silence. ''You really like being an EMT, don't you?''

''I like helping my neighbors,'' he replied. ''Sometimes it's tough, though. Especially if the patient is a child or a friend.''

Dana shook her head. ''I don't think I could do it. I'd panic.''

He met her gaze. ''You didn't panic today.''

''That's because you told me what to do.''

He smiled. ''And you always do what I tell you,'' he teased.

She lifted her chin. ''When it's reasonable.''

''I still wish you'd tell Alison what her fiancé did to you.''

She shook her head. ''It's too late. Besides, I think Clark really has changed.''

''I still say the man is a snake.''

''No, I mean it.'' She told him about Clark's apology at the Valentine's Day Ball. ''And he was a perfect gentleman. No snide innuendos or inappropriate touches. He didn't say or do one thing to make me uncomfortable.''

''That doesn't make him a saint.''

''Of course not. But if alcohol was to blame for his behavior, it explains why he acts so differently now that he's sober. I admire the fact that he's sworn off it. At least he's making an effort to improve.''

He shook his head. ''I can't believe you're sitting here defending that man after what he did to you.''

''I'm not defending what he did,'' she countered. ''But if he's willing to change, then I guess I'm willing to give him a second chance.''

She didn't tell Austin the real reason for her hope for Clark's metamorphosis. Each day as she planned Alison's wedding, the thought that it might end in disaster nagged at her. But if Clark truly had turned over a new leaf, there was every reason to have hope for their marriage.

Dana truly believed in happily ever-afters. That was the reason she'd become a wedding planner in the first place—to make dreams come true.

Austin didn't argue with her anymore, though it was obvious he still didn't trust Clark Oxley or believe he was a new and improved man.

Dana decided to change the subject. ''I enjoyed the stories you told the children today. Were they all true?''

''Every one,'' he said, sounding a little more relaxed now. ''They didn't all happen to me, but when you hire on at a lot of cattle drives, you hear some great stories around the campfire.''

"How long have you been going out on cattle drives?"

"Since I was eighteen," Austin told her. "I left home right after Jack did, since my old man preferred spending more time in the bar than in the barn. He'd sold off all his cattle and leased out the pasture ground, so there was nothing for me there, anyway."

"But you love that ranch. Why didn't he just let you take over?"

He gave her a wry smile. "It's not quite that easy. My old man had delinquent operating loans that he had to pay back. Leasing the land guaranteed a steady income. Turning the ranch over to a cocky teenager who already had some misdemeanors under his belt was a risk no one was willing to take."

"But the ranch is yours now."

"Half of it," Austin reminded her. "I still have to buy the other half from Jack. He's agreed to sell it to me and I think the bank will go for it. They were somewhat gun-shy about loaning me money when I first approached them. Seems I raised a little too much hell in my younger days and they frown on that sort of thing. Puts me in the high-risk-to-default category."

"But you worked it out?"

"I called them yesterday and it looks like they're going to approve the loan."

"Oh, Austin, congratulations," she exclaimed, truly happy for him, even though she knew it meant losing him.

"It's not quite official yet, but I don't anticipate any problems. The neighbor's lease on the pasture ground is up next month, and then the Hawke Ranch will be all mine."

She could hear the pride in his voice. The excitement. "Sounds like you can't wait."

His eyes met hers. "I've been dreaming about this day my entire life, Dana. I want to redeem the Hawke family name. Return the ranch to the way it was when my great-grandfather built it."

Her throat ached as she looked at him. She wanted his dream to come true for him, but she'd probably never know if it did. He'd be gone soon and they'd both move on with their lives. His life in Texas and hers in Seattle.

They'd lose touch with each other. Austin might even forget about these few crazy, precious weeks they'd spent together.

But she would never forget him.

"There's the doctor," he said, rising from the chair. She followed him. Both of them stood slightly apart from Carmen and Amy, but they could overhear the doctor's report.

Carmen braced one arm around a fragile-looking Amy, the girl's eyes red and puffy, her body shaking.

"Your father is in stable condition at the moment," the doctor told her. "He's suffered a cerebral hemorrhage, also known as a stroke."

"Oh, please, no," Amy gasped, shrinking into the older woman.

The emergency room doors opened and Hannah flew inside, her gaze taking in Amy's stricken expression. She turned to Dana. "What happened?"

"Mr. Tidwell's suffered a...stroke," Dana said. The word stuck in her throat.

"Will my dad...be...all right?" Amy asked at last, her gray-blue eyes brimming with tears.

"Only time will tell," the doctor replied gently. "We'll be moving him up to the fourth floor soon. Then you can see him."

Amy gave a shaky nod as the doctor walked away. Then she saw Hannah and her face crumpled once more.

"It will be all right," Hannah said soothingly, taking the young girl into her arms. "Everything will be all right."

Dana knew only too well that might not be true. The days ahead would be rough. Uncertain. Full of ups and downs. She hoped eighteen-year-old Amy Tidwell was strong enough to weather the storm.

Stronger than Dana had been.

Carmen walked over to them. "Thank you so much for everything. Helping Mr. Tidwell and giving me a ride to the hospital."

"No thanks necessary," Austin replied.

"Is there anything else we can do for you or for Amy?" Dana asked.

"No, I think I'll stay here with Amy most of the night," Carmen told them. "You two can go on home."

"Are you sure?" Austin asked.

The older woman gave him a tearful smile as she reached out to squeeze his forearm. "I'm sure. We'll be fine."

Neither Dana nor Austin spoke on the way back to the apartment. A fine mist dropped from the night sky, so the only sound in the cab of the truck was the steady swipe of the windshield wipers against the glass.

"There's snow in the forecast tonight," Austin said

as he pulled into the parking garage. "Light flurries and maybe a little sleet."

Dana looked over at him. "What did you say?"

He frowned. "Is something wrong?"

She pulled her coat more tightly around her. "I'm just cold."

He popped open his door. "Then let's get you inside."

CHAPTER ELEVEN

AUSTIN ADDED ANOTHER LOG to the fire, then returned to the sofa to sit next to Dana, who was now wrapped in a blanket.

"Still cold?" he asked.

"A little."

"Maybe you have a fever." He placed his palm on her forehead, but her skin felt cool to his touch.

"I'm fine," she said, her teeth starting to chatter.

"You're not fine." He scooted closer to her on the sofa, then pulled her into his arms.

"What are you doing?"

"Warming you up the old-fashioned way." He moved under the blanket so her body was flush against his own. She stiffened at first, then relaxed against him, laying her head on his shoulder.

"Did you learn this technique during your EMT training?"

He smiled against her silky hair. It smelled like wild clover honey. "Of course. You don't think I'd take advantage of a situation like this, do you?"

"I certainly hope so," she replied with a sigh.

"Then, why are you still shivering?" he asked, sensing that something was still wrong.

"Today brought back too many memories," Dana said quietly. "Memories I'd rather forget."

His arms tightened around her, and his cheek burrowed against hers. "Tell me."

She didn't say anything for so long that Austin wondered if she'd fallen asleep. But at last she began to speak in a tight, pain-filled voice.

"I was eight years old. We lived in a white house with blue shutters on Meadowlark Lane in Belltown. Nothing big or fancy, but nice, you know?"

He nodded, not wanting to break her flow of words.

"We had a dog named Fizzles," she continued. "He was a springer spaniel who followed me when I rode my bike to school every day." The fire crackled in the hearth as she spoke, shooting a tiny shower of sparks up into the chimney. "Only, one day when I came home, Gram was there and I could see she'd been crying. It scared me, because I'd never seen an adult cry before. She told me something terrible had happened."

Austin closed his eyes, remembering the day his mother was killed in a car accident. His father had cried like a baby until he'd been drunk enough to pass out. Linc had never cried again—at least, not in front of his sons. He'd never stopped drinking, either.

"My father was in the hospital," Dana continued, "and Gram said we had to go there right away."

"Did she tell you why?" he asked.

Dana shook her head. "And I think that scared me more than anything. When we got to the hospital, my mother was there. She was crying, too."

Austin realized that though it might seem like they came from two completely different worlds, in reality, he and Dana shared a common bond—the sudden shattering of an innocent childhood.

"Mom told me my father was sick," Dana continued, "and that I shouldn't be scared when I saw him because he looked…different."

His mind flew back to the day of his mother's funeral. He had come upon her open casket unintentionally after turning a corner in the unfamiliar church. It was apparently common practice to leave it open until the service began, so friends and relatives coming in from out of town could view the body of the deceased.

"Then they took me into his hospital room." Dana's voice was almost a whisper. "The first thing I noticed was the smell. A nauseating, antiseptic odor that to this day I can remember. I saw my dad lying on the bed, hooked up to a bunch of machines. He looked different. Smaller."

He held her tighter, wishing he could make the pain of old memories go away for both of them.

"Then my mother started crying again," Dana said. "She told me I should kiss him goodbye because he might not make it." She sucked in a deep breath. "I was terrified to go near that man in the bed. He wasn't my daddy. My daddy was big and strong and always cracking jokes. The man in the bed was a stranger."

"So what did you do?" Austin asked.

"I ran." A sob racked her. "I ran out of the hospital room as fast as I could. A nurse nabbed me in the hallway and asked me what was wrong, but I couldn't tell her. I was too afraid she'd make me go back in that room again."

"You were only eight," he reminded her gently.

"I know." She sighed. "Gram came out of the room and took me down to the cafeteria for a soda. She told me my father had something wrong with his brain and might not be the same again. It was an aneurysm, though she didn't use that word at the time. And she told me I didn't have to kiss him if I didn't want to. That no matter what, my daddy knew I loved him.''

''I think I would have liked your Gram,'' Austin said.

''She was wonderful.'' Dana shifted on the sofa to face him, her eyes bright with tears. ''But our lives were never the same after that day. My father survived, but his recuperation was painfully slow. My mother had to quit work to take care of him. With no health insurance, we had to sell the house to pay our bills. That's when we moved to the trailer. I lost my old school and my old friends. Even Fizzles.''

''You couldn't take your dog with you when you moved?''

''We did, but he got hit by a car one day after following me to my new school.''

''You saw it happen?''

She shook her head. ''I found out about it when I came home from school. My mother was crying again. She cried a lot after my dad got sick.''

''Did he ever recover?''

''Not completely. He never was quite the same after the aneurysm—never strong again. My mother eventually went back to work, but the bills had piled up, so we had to stay in the trailer park. You know, it really wasn't so bad. I liked the people there. But it changed the way other people looked at us.''

''People like Clark,'' he said tightly.

Her molten gray gaze met his own. ''Yes. We were trailer-park trash. That's what the kids at school called me. The 'popular' kids, anyway. My mother kept assuring me they'd mature as they grew up, and stop acting like that by the time we all reached high school, but it didn't happen.''

''That's why it was so important to impress those people at the Highland Country Club? To prove to them that you're just as good as they are?''

''No,'' she said, meeting his gaze, her own eyes wide with sudden understanding. ''I think I wanted to prove it to myself.''

''And did you?'' he asked softly, admiring her honesty. Hell, at this moment, Austin couldn't think of anything he didn't like about her.

She gave a slow nod. ''But the most amazing thing I discovered was that Alison and her friends didn't even remember me. After all the hell they put me through, all the time I'd spent dreaming of ways to take revenge when I was rich and famous, it was like it had never happened. For them, anyway.''

''But not for you,'' he reminded her. ''I still don't understand why you would want to plan the wedding of two people who made you so miserable.''

''What does it matter now? This job is almost over. I'm meeting with Alison at the Palace Hotel at one o'clock tomorrow, and the next time we get together will be her wedding.'' She smiled. ''Besides, I realize now that my mother was right. Alison and Clark have matured.''

''I still wish I'd hit him when I had the chance,'' he muttered.

She laughed. ''That doesn't sound very mature.''

He grinned, happy to see her smiling again.

''But it sure sounds satisfying.''

"I'll admit I was tempted, too, the first time I saw him again," she confessed, leaning her head against his shoulder. "Because I'd given him too much power over me. The power to make me dislike myself."

Austin brushed his cheek against her hair, amazed at how perfectly she fit against him. "Does he still have that power?"

She sat up to face him. "No. I like the woman I've become."

"So do I," he said huskily. "Too much."

He wasn't ready to admit that his feelings for her went even deeper. That he was falling in love with her.

Something evocative gleamed in her eyes. "And that's a problem?"

"Hell, yes, it's a problem," he replied, trying to convince himself as much as her. We're complete opposites."

She smiled. "Because you like beefsteak and I'm a sushi kind of girl?"

"Because you thrive in the big city and I like wide-open spaces."

"And the only mustang I've ever ridden is a car."

"Complete opposites," he said, his gaze dropping to her lush, pink mouth.

"In every way," she agreed, leaning closer.

"So what the hell are we doing," he whispered against her mouth.

"Playing with fire," she breathed, before nibbling his lower lip.

He groaned low in his throat, sinking into her for a mind-blowing kiss. Her fingers furrowed his hair, her nails lightly scoring his scalp. Then she moved against him, her body shifting against his groin, and the fire inside of him threatened to burst into an inferno.

The sofa hampered his movements, so without breaking the kiss, he rolled off it, landing on the floor with Dana on top of him.

He liked her there. She sat up, her legs cradling his hips and her hands on his shirt.

"Now I have you exactly where I want you," she teased, her eyes darkening with desire.

"And what are you going to do about it?" he challenged, his body throbbing.

She flicked the top button of his shirt open, then the next. "I'm going to show you how a city girl makes love."

His breath hitched at her words. "I can't wait."

"You're going to have to wait, cowboy," she said, tugging his shirt out of his jeans, "because I'm the one in charge now."

"I think there's one thing you should know about cowboys," he said as she spread his shirt open.

"What?" she asked, bending down to kiss his chest, then licking at one nipple.

He rolled over so she lay beneath him, her gray eyes hooded with desire and anticipation. "We can make love all night long."

"Prove it," she challenged.

So he did.

DANA AWOKE THE NEXT DAY to find herself in her bed, Austin's big, warm body flush against her own. Sometime during the night he had carried her there, then proceeded to make slow, sweet love to her again. And again.

She smiled to herself as she leaned up to brush her lips against the rough whiskers on his square chin. He was sound asleep, though the sun filtering through the window shade told her it was long past sunrise.

She and her cowboy had made love until dawn before finally falling into a sated sleep. Dana stretched luxuriously under the cotton sheets, her body a little sore in all the right places.

Glancing at the clock, she was surprised to find it even later than she thought. Almost noon. She had a one o'clock meeting with Alison at the Palace Hotel.

For a moment, she thought about postponing it so she could stay in bed with Austin all day. But the meeting would take less than an hour. She could probably be home and back under the covers before Austin even awoke.

Carefully lifting the sheet, she slipped out of bed, her bare feet sinking silently into the plush carpet. She turned to look at Austin, his face completely relaxed in slumber, one broad hand cradling the pillow under his head. Her body tingled when she remembered everything he'd done with those hands the night before.

She'd never met any man like him before and she knew in her heart that she never would again. He was the one. The man she'd been waiting for all her life. Gram had always told her she'd know when the right man came along.

The realization hadn't come with an explosion of fireworks, but rather a quiet recognition deep in her soul. As if Austin had been the perfect man for her all along, but she'd finally opened her eyes to see it.

Just like he'd helped Dana to see—and like—herself.

With a contented sigh, she gathered up her clothes, then padded silently to the bathroom. Twenty minutes later, she was ready to go. Slipping on her shoes, she realized she'd have to take a taxi. They had called a tow truck for her car last night, and Austin's pickup was a stick-shift, which she didn't know how to drive.

By the time the taxi pulled up at the Palace Hotel, Dana was fully awake. But instead of thinking about work, her mind kept drifting back to Austin. She ascended the elevator to the floor of office suites, hoping Alison wouldn't be upset that she was running a few minutes late.

She knocked on the door of suite 407 and it opened a moment later.

Clark Oxley stood on the other side of the threshold. "Good morning, Dana. We'd almost given up on you."

"Sorry I'm late," she replied, walking inside and setting down her briefcase. She hadn't expected both Clark and Alison to be here. Of course, his family did own this hotel. Perhaps he worked out of an office on the same floor.

"Where's Alison?" Dana asked, shrugging out of her trench coat as she looked around the well-appointed suite. There were two large rooms separated by an open archway.

"Alison won't be joining us."

She turned around to see Clark flipping the lock on the door. Ice filled her veins when she caught the expression on his face.

"What's going on?" she breathed.

"I think you know, Dana." He wobbled a little as he walked toward her, and now she could smell the alcohol on his breath. "It's time to finish what we started ten years ago."

AUSTIN FORCED HIS eyelids open as a loud ringing reverberated around him. One hand reached out and fumbled for the telephone on the nightstand. He knocked the receiver to the floor, then leaned over to pick it up and place it against his ear.

"Hello?" he said, his eyes only half open.

"Austin?" asked a chipper voice on the other end of the line. "Is that you?"

He fell back against the pillow, suddenly aware that he was in bed alone. "Yeah?"

"This is Alison Van Hoek. How are you?"

Tired. Happy. In love. "I'm just fine, Alison. What can I do for you?"

"May I speak to Dana?"

"Hold on," he said, climbing out of bed. "I'll see if I can find her."

He set down the phone, then pulled on his jeans and went in search of the woman he'd held in his arms all night long. Their lovemaking had been incredible.

Dana was incredible.

He'd tried to convince himself that his attraction to her was only physical, but last night proved how much more she meant to him. He loved her deeply. That was the only way to explain the funny ache in his chest when he couldn't find her anywhere in the apartment.

"I'm sorry, I guess she's not here," he said when he picked up the receiver again. Then something clicked in his head. "Hey, isn't she supposed to be meeting you in your office this morning?"

Alison laughed. "I don't think so. I'm at a design

conference in New York City that's been on my schedule for weeks. I won't be back in Seattle until late tomorrow afternoon.''

How was that possible? Dana had told him last night that she had a meeting with Alison at one o'clock. *But she didn't say who had arranged that meeting.*

Austin picked up his watch off the nightstand. The digital display read twelve-fifteen. Apprehension filled him when he thought of one possible explanation. The only one that made sense.

''I've got to go,'' he said into the phone.

''Wait, I—''

But Austin dropped the receiver and ran out of the bedroom, grabbing his shirt on the way. His head told him not to panic, that he was probably overreacting. But the pounding of his heart warned him that something was very wrong.

He just hoped he wasn't already too late.

DANA STARED AT CLARK, not wanting to believe the obvious. He'd tricked her into coming here. Alison had never scheduled this meeting—it had been a ploy for Clark to get her alone. A ploy that had worked all too well.

''Why are you doing this?'' she asked.

''Because I've found that the old attraction is still there,'' Clark replied, his eyes slightly unfocussed. It was obvious he'd had far too much to drink. ''I've tried to fight it, but I find something about you simply irresistible.''

His preternatural calmness unnerved her. ''Let me go, Clark.''

He smiled as he pulled a serving cart out of the other

room. "Not yet. I've ordered us some brunch. Just sit down and relax. Give me a chance to make my pitch."

She watched him remove a bottle of champagne from the ice bucket, then grab a corkscrew. Dana wondered if she was having a nightmare.

The cork popped, telling her this was all too real. Clark filled two champagne flutes with the sparkling wine and handed one to Dana. She took it, her mind scrambling for some way to extricate herself from this situation. Some way to reason with him.

"You told me you gave up drinking," she said.

He took a sip from his glass. "I told you a lot of things I thought you wanted to hear. Women like to be wooed, don't they? To believe a man would sacrifice just for her."

He was delusional. "I never thought you did it for me."

"But I did," he said, moving closer to her. "I like you, Dana. I've always liked you. Can't you see that? I just want us to be friends."

His patronizing tone made her flesh crawl. "A friend wouldn't try to trick me. Or lock me in a hotel suite with him."

"There's no need to panic," Clark assured her. "Just give me a chance to convince you that we could be good together. Very good."

"You're marrying Alison in three days," Dana reminded him, growing more desperate. The man seemed to have no conscience. No regard for her feelings.

Just like in high school.

The same helpless feelings she'd had then threatened to overwhelm her now. But she had to stay in control. She refused to let him have that kind of power over her again.

Which meant she had to find a way to help herself. For now, the best way to do that was to keep him talking.

"Alison will be my wife," Clark said, "but you can be part of my life, too."

"In what way?" Dana asked, her mouth parched. She took a small sip of the champagne, trying to keep her hand steady. How could she have misjudged him? Austin had been right about him all along.

"In every way. Just think of all the advantages I can give you if we become…closer. I've got a lot of friends in high places, Dana. And something tells me those are places you want to go."

Clark obviously believed money and prestige to be potent aphrodisiacs. Dana couldn't deny that she had been fighting for both. That at one time, she had wanted to be part of Clark and Alison's world.

But not anymore.

She definitely preferred Austin's honest integrity to Clark's oily manipulations. Her cowboy might not be rich or powerful, but he was a better man than Clark Oxley would ever be.

"How about some more champagne?" Clark offered, holding up the bottle.

"Yes, please," she said, rising and holding out her glass. "Because I'd like to propose a toast."

He smiled as he topped off her glass, smug satisfaction shining in his eyes. "I can't wait to hear it."

She raised her glass high in the air. "To Clark Oxley, the man who has everything—and is still the biggest loser I've ever known."

His face darkened as he carefully set down his glass. "So I take it you're not interested in my offer?"

"To become your mistress? No." She put her glass down on the end table, telling herself not to show any fear. Cowards like Clark Oxley fed off fear. She turned to leave.

"I don't think you understand." He moved to block her path. "I want you, Dana. And I always get what I want."

Then he lunged at her, propelling her back onto the sofa. He was on her in an instant, his lanky body pressing down hard on hers as his mouth sought her lips.

She placed her palms against his chest and pushed hard, but he was deceptively strong, his fingers digging into her collarbone as he held her down.

"My sexy little trailer-park tramp," he murmured, nuzzling her neck.

Anger welled up inside her as she fought him off. But he forced her down on the sofa again, using his weight to contain her. She cried out, but his thick lips covered hers, cutting off the sound. She bit down hard on his invading tongue, and he reared back in pain.

At that moment, a hard *bang* sounded against the door of the suite. Another one quickly followed, and the wood splintered, leaving the door barely hanging by the hinges.

Then she saw Austin standing at the threshold.

CHAPTER TWELVE

AUSTIN STOOD THERE, his shoulders heaving from the exertion of knocking the door down. Then he saw Clark on top of Dana and exploded into the room.

Clark stood up and backed away from Dana, holding both hands up in front of him. "Now, hold on just a minute," he said.

But Dana could see Austin was past the point of listening. His fist stopped Clark's mouth from saying another word. An uppercut to his chin made the man fall back hard on the carpet.

But Austin simply hauled him up by his shirt collar and hit him again. This time a bone-cracking blow to the midsection.

Clark tried to fight back, but his flailing fists hit nothing but air. He was outmatched and outclassed.

"Please," Clark begged, blood streaming out of one nostril and his eyes tearing up.

Austin hesitated, his fists still tightly clenched. Then Dana saw a shadow of movement behind him. She'd been so intent on the fight, she hadn't seen the two burly security guards walk through the door.

Before she could shout out a warning, one of them struck Austin on the side of his head with a nightstick. Her cowboy dropped straight to his knees, his gray eyes rolling back in their sockets.

"Austin," she cried, running over to try to break his fall. But the security guards held her back. Austin collapsed onto the carpet and didn't move.

"Took you long enough," Clark muttered, grabbing a white linen napkin off the serving table to staunch the flow of blood from his nose.

"We came as soon as we heard the alarm," one guard replied, nodding toward the broken door.

Dana struggled in their grasp. "Please let me go!"

Austin lay on the floor unmoving, his face unnaturally pale except for the rapidly swelling purple bruise on the side of his head. For a moment, she feared they'd killed him. Then she saw the rise and fall of his chest, and relief tore through her. He wasn't dead, just unconscious.

One of the security guards turned to Clark. "Should I call the police?"

"Yes," Dana cried, fear for Austin fueling her rage.

Clark ignored her outburst, daubing at his nose and gingerly manipulating his jaw. "Leave us alone for a moment. I need to have a short discussion with Ms. Ulrich."

"No," Dana blurted, alarmed at being left alone with Clark again, although he looked as if he was hardly able to stand, much less attack her. He was bent over slightly at the waist, wincing with every raspy breath.

The security guards hesitated, then abruptly let Dana go. She fell onto her knees on the carpet and moved next to Austin, then gently cradled his head in her hands. His skin was warm to her touch, and the rhythm of his breathing seemed normal.

"Just wait out in the hall," Clark ordered them. "And call somebody about fixing the damn door."

When they were out of sight, Dana looked up at Clark. "You're not getting away with it this time!"

Her threat didn't seem to scare him. "Let's be logical about this."

Dana scooped up some ice from the ice bucket and rolled it in a napkin. Then she placed it gently against Austin's head. He was still out cold. "Listen to logic from a man who just tried to attack me? I don't think so."

"That's your story," he replied evenly. "I'll say you conned me in to meeting here for a romantic rendezvous and your jealous boyfriend burst in on us and went crazy."

"That's not true!"

"The police will believe it," he countered. "Especially if those two security officers come forward as witnesses and verify my version of events."

"They'd lie for you?"

"Lying is in the eye of the beholder," Clark said, his breath still ragged. "A lot like love. You think I shouldn't marry Alison because I happen to be attracted to you. But I do love her and I will make her happy."

Austin groaned, drawing her attention away from Clark. When she saw that he was starting to regain consciousness, she almost wept with gratitude.

"The Oxley name carries a lot of weight in this city," Clark continued, ignoring the semiconscious man at his feet. "No offense, but the Ulrich name hasn't much clout."

As much as she hated to admit it, he was right. Why

would the police believe her over an Oxley? Especially if he had witnesses—*his employees*—to back him up.

"All the cops have to do is take one look at me," he added. "It's obvious I'm the one who's the victim here."

"And what about this?" she asked, pulling away the collar of her blouse to reveal the small bruises he'd inflicted when he'd held her down on the sofa.

"Who's to say your boyfriend didn't do that? The man's an animal. He deserves to go to jail. But it's up to you to make that decision, Dana. If you press charges against me, I press charges against him. It's that simple." His eyes narrowed. "But I guarantee you that I can make mine stick."

He sounded so sure. So confident. Dana's head spun, and her knees were still wobbly from the surprise attack. She needed time to think. Not that Clark had left her much choice.

"Nothing changes," he stated. "You don't tell Alison. You keep planning the wedding. And everyone lives happily ever after."

Nausea welled up inside her. She couldn't let Clark get away with this. But how could she stop him? She remembered Austin telling her about his police record. They were only misdemeanors—but would that matter to a judge?

Just the fact that he was arrested might hinder Austin's ability to secure that loan for his ranch. He'd told her himself that the banker had been hesitant to lend him the money because of his past.

Austin could lose the ranch he loved because of her. Because she'd been too blind, too driven by ambition to listen to him.

"If you ever try to touch me again," Dana said, her voice shaking with anger, "I swear I will kill you myself."

"Don't worry," he sneered, holding one arm across his rib cage. "I've suddenly lost my appetite for trailer trash. So, do we have a deal?"

"Yes." She was caught in the web of deceit he'd spun for her. Dana loved Austin enough to protect him.

Even if it meant losing him.

THE DRONE OF VOICES penetrated his throbbing head and Austin opened his eyes to see where they were coming from. The room was blurry at first, then suddenly cleared. He saw Dana sitting right by his side, her sweet scent penetrating his nostrils.

Then Clark Oxley came into view, towering over him. He struggled to sit up, but dark spots flashed before his eyes.

Dana laid one hand on his shoulder to steady him. He sucked in a deep breath, unable to get to his feet yet. So he propped his back against an overstuffed armchair, fighting off another wave of dizziness.

"Are you all right?" Austin asked her, his voice sounding hoarse to his ears.

Tears gleamed in her eyes. "Yes. Are you?"

"I have one hell of a headache."

"You deserve a lot worse," Clark said, tossing a bloody linen napkin onto the floor. "Dana came here to see me of her own free will. You had no reason to burst in here like some deranged knight in shining armor."

Dana was strangely silent beside him. He noticed two champagne glasses on the table by the sofa, both half empty, as well as a serving cart with silver chafing dishes.

"What's really going on?" he asked her.

She looked at him, her throat contracting, but she didn't say a word.

"I know what I saw," Austin persisted. "I heard you cry out."

Clark took a step closer to Dana. "Passion can do that to a woman."

Austin didn't want to believe him, but Dana wasn't saying anything to contradict the jerk. Despite the pain in his head, he tried to think back to exactly what he'd seen when he'd come through that door. Dana lying on the sofa. Clark on top of her.

Had they been struggling? He honestly couldn't remember; his mind was still too fuzzy. But Austin did remember the way he and Dana had made love last night. That had been very real.

What Clark was telling him now had to be a lie.

"Why are you covering for him?" Austin asked her, silently pleading for her to tell him what he wanted to hear. That she hadn't chosen Oxley over him, even if the man could give her everything she'd ever wanted.

"That's sweet," Clark jeered. "You still don't get it, do you, Hawke? Dana picked me. Although I think she does have a soft spot for you. You must remind her of home."

She shot to her feet. "Stop it."

Austin tried to stand up, nausea gripping his gut. "Dana, for the last time, tell me what's going on here."

She sucked in a deep breath. "Clark already told you."

He stared at her. "It can't be true."

"Of course it's true," Clark replied, reaching for his jacket. "Do you really expect Dana to throw away her career and her business for some renegade cowboy, when she can have someone like me in her life?"

She met Austin's gaze, tears in her eyes. "I'm sorry." Then she turned and ran out of the suite.

Austin watched her go, feeling as if someone had just cold-cocked him again.

Two security guards appeared in the doorway.

"Escort Mr. Hawke out of the hotel," Clark ordered, picking up a champagne flute and raising it to his swollen mouth. "And make sure he stays out."

Austin barely registered the ride down the elevator. The next thing he knew he was out on the sidewalk, a light drizzle falling on him. He brushed the wetness out of his eyes, cringing when he touched the bump on the side of his head. But his mind was surprisingly clear.

It was time to go home.

DANA WALKED TEN BLOCKS, her tears mingling with the rain. Part of her wanted to track down Austin and tell him the truth. But to what purpose? He'd just go after Clark again, risking everything that mattered to him.

She shivered as she walked, realizing too late that she'd left her trench coat in the suite, along with her briefcase. No way would she return to the Palace Hotel and risk running into Clark again. He was probably licking his wounds. It would be bad enough when she had to face him at the wedding on Friday. But she couldn't think about that now.

The wind hit her as she turned the corner. Thankfully, it was only a few more blocks back to her apartment.

It can't be true.

Austin's words reverberated in her head. The stricken expression on his face had torn a hole in her heart. He didn't want to believe her so shallow. So selfish. But what else could he think?

She loved him too much to let him sacrifice himself for her. If Clark pressed charges against him, there was a very good chance Austin would end up in jail.

If only her grandmother were still alive. She needed to talk to someone who might understand. Hailing a taxi, Dana climbed into the warm cab, then gave him the address of a place she hadn't been to in a very long time.

When the cab pulled into the trailer park, Dana barely had enough money in her pocket to pay the fare. The driver snarled at her for not giving him a tip, then peeled away, spitting gravel in his wake.

Dana turned to the pale pink double-wide trailer that had been her home for so many years. They were still white lace curtains in the windows, and a dried eucalyptus wreath hung on the door.

The creaking porch steps announced her arrival, and her mother had the door open before she even knocked. "Dana, what a nice surprise!"

"I haven't seen you in a while," Dana said, stepping inside. The place smelled the same, like cinnamon cider. There was a kettle of it simmering on the stove and the familiar scent made her feel a little better.

"I know, it's been much too long," Connie Ulrich

said. "Now, come into the kitchen and warm up. You're absolutely soaked."

"It's raining out," Dana replied, stating the obvious. There was a steady patter on the roof of the trailer home. That was one of the things she remembered most about living here, the tremendous noise a storm made as it battered the aluminum siding of the trailer from all sides.

Connie pulled a bulky sweater from the closet and wrapped it around her daughter's shoulders. "Don't you own an umbrella? You could catch pneumonia on a wet, cold day like this."

A smile haunted her lips. "Mom, you're nagging."

Connie kissed the top of her head. "I guess old habits are hard to break."

Dana brushed her wet hair off her forehead as her mother poured them each a cup of steaming cider.

"So what's new in your life?" Connie sat across the table from her. "I haven't seen you since Christmas—before that awful article appeared in *Seattle Magazine*. I hope it didn't have a negative effect on your business."

Where to begin. She hadn't wanted to burden her mother with her career woes, so she'd kept her distance. A decision she regretted now.

Picking up the cup in front of her, she blew on it gently. "Business has slowed down quite a bit, although I do have a wedding coming up this weekend."

Connie watched her daughter. "You don't seem very happy about it."

The sip of cider Dana took burned its way down her throat. "It's been…difficult."

"In what way?"

Dana hesitated. She'd never told her parents or Gram exactly what Clark Oxley had done to her in high school. She'd wanted to spare them the shame and humiliation she'd endured. "The bride and groom graduated with me from Westwood High."

"Oh." Her mother didn't need to hear more. She knew how unhappy Dana had been in high school. "So it brought back some old memories."

Dana nodded. "Can I ask you a question, Mom?"

"Sure."

"How come you never moved? I mean, you're working full time now at the nursing home. You could afford a nice apartment in a decent neighborhood."

She shrugged. "I like it here, Dana. I've made good friends."

"You don't ever want something...more?"

Connie considered her question. At last she said, "When you work with hospice patients, you hear what's really important in their lives. What they're going to miss the most when they're gone. It's never a house or a car or a boat. Rarely a job or an elected position. It's always people. Family and friends."

"Like Gram," Dana said softly. "I miss her so much."

Connie's eyes misted. "Me, too."

Dana stared down at her cup. "I messed up, Mom. And I don't know how to fix it."

"Sometimes fixing it isn't an option," Connie said. "You just have to live with it or move on."

Neither alternative appealed to her. But maybe her mother was right. Dana had made her choice. Now she just had to live with it.

"Do you want to tell me about your problem?" Connie stood up and placed her empty cup in the sink. "I have about thirty minutes before my shift starts."

"Thanks," Dana replied, "but I think I'd better figure out this one on my own."

Connie patted her shoulder. "You let me know if you change your mind."

"I will," Dana promised. "But would you mind giving me a lift to Brader's Auto Shop? The Beast stalled again yesterday, but it should be ready to go now."

"Sure, it's right on my way." Connie grabbed two coats out of the closet, handing the extra one to her daughter.

"Thanks, Mom," Dana said, putting it on.

"That's one problem solved, anyway." She leaned over to kiss Dana's cheek. "Don't worry so much about the others. Sometimes they have a way of resolving themselves."

When Dana arrived back at her apartment, she slipped the key into the lock, her stomach in knots. What if Austin was inside waiting for her? Demanding details about what exactly had happened this afternoon in that hotel suite? Dana wasn't sure she could keep up the charade. If he really wanted to hear the answers, she'd give them to him.

But the living room was dark when she opened the front door. Austin wasn't in the living room or the kitchen or the bathroom. She opened the closet door to find his bedroll and suitcase had disappeared. Then she saw his apartment key on the coffee table, and her heart sank.

Another problem solved. Austin was gone.

And he wasn't coming back.

JACK WALKED INTO the microbrewery, his eyes adjusting to the dimness as he searched for his brother.

He finally saw Austin hunkered over a beer at the far end of the bar.

He walked over and slid onto the bar stool next to him, noting the ugly, swollen bruise on the side of his head. "You look like hell."

"Thanks." Austin took a sip of his beer. "I feel worse."

"Must be a woman."

"Lucky guess."

"Not really. Last time you looked like this you had started a brawl in a Texas honky-tonk."

Austin flexed his right hand, the knuckles slightly swollen. "I'm a lot classier now. This time I started a brawl in the Palace Hotel."

Jack stared at him. "You're serious?"

"Well, brawl might be an exaggeration. The other guy didn't put up much of a fight."

"So who was the other guy?"

"Clark Oxley."

It took a moment for the name to sink in. "*The* Clark Oxley?"

"Please don't tell me there are two of them," Austin said wryly.

Jack only knew of one, but he was powerful enough for ten men. The Oxley family name was big in both the Seattle business world and local politics. "You sure do know how to pick 'em."

"Are you talking about sparring partners or women?"

"Looks like both," Jack replied. "So what happened?"

"Same old thing. I walked into a room and saw another guy with my girl. Instead of stopping to ask questions, I let my fists do the talking."

"Dana and Clark?" Jack asked incredulously.

"Why not?" Austin asked, bitterness seeping into his voice. "He's rich. Powerful. A big man in this city. Every woman's dream."

"He's also engaged to be married in just a few days." Jack knew his brother had a jealous streak a mile wide. "Look, Austin, you were wrong ten years ago when you thought I was moving in on your girl. Did you ever consider the possibility that you might be wrong again?"

"I'm not," he said firmly.

"Don't make the same mistake I did," Jack warned him. "Stay and fight for the woman you love."

"I already did." Austin's jaw tightened. "She still picked the other guy."

"Now what?" Jack asked, sensing his brother's pride had been badly bruised, along with his head and heart.

"Now I'm going back to Texas. That's why I called you. The wedding plans are almost finished, so I kept up my end of the bargain. If you need anything else from me, you know all you have to do is call."

"Why are you going back?" Jack challenged. "To drown your pain in a bottle, like the old man?"

"I'm going back because that's where I belong." Austin pushed his beer away, then swiveled on the stool to face his brother. "I don't belong here, Jack. That was made crystal clear to me today, although it took a blow to the head to finally see it."

"You're too damn stubborn," Jack muttered, knowing nothing he said would make any difference.

In many ways, Austin hadn't changed in the past ten years. His little brother felt things deeply, he always had. Although at six feet three inches, Austin could hardly be called little. He played the tough guy well, but his wounds took a long time to heal. And this one went straight to the heart.

"It's genetic," Austin replied. "Remember?"

"Yeah. I also remember you just offered to let me call you if I needed anything. Well, I do need something."

"What?"

"I need you to stand up as my best man."

Austin gave a brisk nod. "I'd be honored."

"So, you'll come back for the wedding?"

"Hell, yes, Jack. You're family."

Jack swallowed, regretting the fact that he'd let ten years slip by without even bothering to call his brother. There was no way he'd ever let it happen again.

"Promise me you won't hide out on that ranch, Austin. There are a lot of ways to run away from life. I see it in my work as a parole officer every day. Dad chose the bottle. Some people choose drugs or crime. If I know you, work will be your escape. Just don't let it keep you from living."

Austin smiled, though the small movement seemed to cause him some pain. "Hell, Jack, now you sound just like a preacher."

At least his brother hadn't lost his sense of humor. "All right, no more sermons. Just think about what I said."

"Will you say goodbye to Adam and Hannah for me?"

"Sure," Jack said, suddenly realizing how much he was going to miss Austin.

"I'll be back a couple of days before the wedding," Austin promised. "Like I said, if you need anything before then…"

"I'll know where to find you," Jack finished for him. "Are you leaving today?"

Austin fished a couple of bills out of his wallet and tossed them onto the bar. "No reason to stay."

"Are you sure you want to end it this way with Dana?" Jack still found it hard to believe the woman had dumped his brother. Something wasn't right.

"I'm not sure about anything anymore." Then he was gone.

Jack stared at the door, resisting the urge to run after him. Austin was a grown man now, not his baby brother. He didn't need Jack to protect him.

Even from himself.

CHAPTER THIRTEEN

THE DAY OF THE VAN HOEK wedding dawned clear and bright. Dana arrived at Our Lady of Mercy Church early Friday afternoon to make certain everything was prepared for the ceremony.

She hadn't heard from Austin since he moved out of the apartment. Assuming he'd gone back to his brother's houseboat, she'd picked up the phone to call him at least three times. But each time, she'd hung up again before completing the dial. Nothing had changed between them. He'd never understand what had happened in that hotel suite.

And he'd never forgive her.

As Dana moved woodenly through her duties, she wasn't sure she could forgive herself. When Alison arrived at the church, she was almost giddy with excitement. Her bridesmaids, including Nina and Chloe, joined her in the dressing room in the church basement, busily preparing for the six o'clock ceremony.

Dana ran through her checklist, making sure everything was set. Guests had begun to arrive, filling up the church pews. She signaled the organist to start the prelude, then went in search of the candlelighters.

At last the moment arrived to notify the groom and his attendants that it was time for the ceremony to begin. She couldn't stand the thought of seeing Clark's smirk again. Facing him last night at rehearsal had been difficult enough.

So smug because he'd won again.

Realizing she'd delayed long enough, Dana headed for a tiny room off the sanctuary and tapped lightly on the closed door.

"Come on in," a deep male voice called out. "We're decent."

"Speak for yourself," another male quipped, as Dana opened the door.

Her gaze went immediately to Clark, who wore his tuxedo like a second skin. The man was a chameleon, altering his personality and appearance to fit any situation. At this moment, he was playing the anxious groom, checking his watch and smoothing back his blond hair.

"We're about ready to begin," Dana said, reciting the same spiel she used at every wedding. "Just follow the cues from the rehearsal last night and there shouldn't be any problems. And remember not to lock your knees during the ceremony. That cuts off the blood flow and could make you feel faint."

The men nodded, pulling their coats off the back of the chairs and slipping them on.

She breathed a sigh of relief as she left the room, leaving the door ajar behind her. But Clark's jeering voice stopped her in her tracks."

"Listen to the expert," Clark said as she left the room. "If anyone knows about not locking your knees, it's Dana Ulrich."

The sound of male laughter made heat wash up her cheeks, but she couldn't move.

"You've done it with the wedding planner?" asked an incredulous voice.

Dana leaned against the wall and closed her eyes, humiliated. None of the other men in there knew her, except Clark's best man Phillip Brandt, who had attended Westwood High.

"I knew her back in high school," Clark said. "She's come up in the world since then, but believe me, she was one hot little trailer-park tramp. If you boys play your cards right, one of you might get lucky tonight." Then he laughed. "Or maybe all of you."

The laughter was more subdued now, but Dana barely heard it. The door squeaked open and she slipped around the corner to avoid them. Anger consumed her, burning away the last of her flimsy excuses. There was no way she could stand by and let this wedding proceed. For Alison's sake. For her own sake.

She had been telling herself that she'd kept quiet because no one would believe her. That she'd gone along with Clark's blackmail scheme to protect Austin. But the truth was that she'd done it to protect herself, too.

To protect her career. But how could she ever respect herself again if she let Clark get away with this?

The reverberations of the pipe organ heralded the first notes of Wagner's "Wedding March." Dana took off down the back hallway, knowing she had to stop Alison before it was too late.

She hastily wound her way through the narrow, hidden passages that led to the back of the sanctuary, arriving just in time to see Alison and her father start down the aisle. Gasping for breath, she watched as the picture-perfect ceremony she'd planned unfolded before her eyes. The guests rose in unison as the bride walked happily toward her groom.

Then it began.

"My dear friends, we have come together in this church…"

Dana watched Clark smile at his bride. A confident smile. And why not? Hadn't he told Dana that he always got what he wanted?

"Who gives this woman to this man…"

Dana had been living in fear, afraid to trust herself. Afraid to trust Austin with the truth. He might not have told Dana that he loved her, but he'd shown her in so many wonderful ways.

She wanted to prove herself worthy of that love. To finally do the right thing.

"If any one of you can show just cause why they may not lawfully be married, let him speak now, or else forever hold your peace.…"

Dana stepped forward and said in a loud, clear voice, "I do."

Shocked gasps and furtive whispers surrounded her as she walked up the aisle, treading pink rose petals under her shoes. She kept moving, her heart pounding in her chest. This was the most outrageous thing she'd done in her life. And the most necessary.

Alison's father half rose from his seat in the front pew, his face livid. "What the hell is going on here?"

Dana walked right past him and up the three steps to the altar.

Alison turned to her, completely bewildered. "Dana, what on earth are you doing?"

Clark glared at her.

The elderly priest, Father LoBianco, cleared his throat, obviously surprised at this unexpected turn of events. "You wish to make an objection?"

Dana nodded, even as Alison's eyes filled tears. "I'm afraid I do."

"You're ruining my wedding," she cried in a hushed whisper. "Please go away!"

"I'm so sorry," she said, knowing her attempt to enlighten Alison about her groom would probably be futile. The ceremony would go on without her. Dana's career would be over after today.

"Get her out of here," Clark muttered to his best man, who now moved in her direction.

But the priest intercepted him. "Perhaps the three of us should retire to my office for a moment and settle this matter in private."

"But this is my wedding," Alison cried, as the murmurs of the crowd grew even louder behind them. "This can't be happening to me."

"Please," Father LoBianco said, motioning toward a back door off to the side of the altar. "The sooner we settle this, the sooner we can resume the ceremony."

Alison shoved her bouquet into the maid of honor's hands, then lifted the skirts of her gown and marched toward the back of the sanctuary.

Clark followed her, his jaw set.

The priest turned to Dana. "I hope you realize how serious this is, young lady."

She nodded. "Believe me, I know."

When all three of them were in the office, the priest closed the door, then turned to Dana. "What are your objections to this wedding?"

Now that the moment had arrived, Dana had trouble finding the right words, giving Clark just enough time to go on the offensive.

"We might as well get this all out in the open," Clark said, turning to Alison. "Honey, I know what this is all about. Dana came on to me the other day, and when I turned her down, she swore she would make me pay." He shook his head. "But even I didn't think she would go this far."

"That's not true!" Dana cried. "Clark attacked me. That's why I had to stop this wedding. He did it when we were in high school and tried it again three days ago."

Alison looked from her fiancé to Dana and back again, her eyes registering her shock. "You're each claiming the other came on to you?"

"Clark did more than come on to me," Dana replied, her entire body shaking. This was harder than she'd ever imagined. "He locked me in your office suite at the Palace Hotel and tried to force himself on me."

Alison took a step away from her. "You're insane!"

Clark nodded, placing one arm around Alison's waist. "Now I think we know why she's called the wedding jinx. She's so twisted and bitter she can't stand to see anyone else happy."

Dana ignored him, focusing her full attention on Alison. She was the one who needed to hear the truth. After that, if she still wanted to marry Clark, so be it.

"Clark told me you wanted to meet me at your suite at one o'clock last Tuesday afternoon," Dana began. "But when I got there, he was the only one inside. He locked the door before I realized what he intended to do. Then he made it very clear that he wanted me to be his mistress.''

"Oh, please," Clark exclaimed. "She propositioned me for money. I'll bet her bank statement is in the red."

He was trying to poke holes in her story, shred her credibility before she could even finish. But she wasn't about to let him sidetrack her.

"He poured us both a glass of champagne," she continued. "When I asked him to let me go, he refused."

Alison sagged into a chair, her face pinched. "This can't be happening."

Dana took a deep breath. "Before he could go any further, Austin burst into the room. Somehow he had figured out what was happening. I never found out how."

Alison looked up at her. "You said this happened last Tuesday?"

She nodded. "Yes, but Clark did the same thing to me in high school—only, that time I was trapped in a car with him. I managed to escape, but no one would believe that Clark Oxley would do such a thing."

"Because it's not true," Clark said through clenched teeth. "Father Dom, can't you do something to stop this?"

"Let the girl finish," the priest said quietly, his face revealing nothing.

Dana kept her gaze on the bride. "I have nothing to gain by telling you this, Alison, and everything to lose. My career. My business. I've already lost Austin."

"I'd like her to come up with one iota of proof,"

Clark said in a dangerously low voice, "to back up these ludicrous allegations."

"I don't have any proof," Dana admitted. "Just my word."

"Why now?" Alison breathed, her face as white as her dress. "Why didn't you tell me all of this before today?"

Dana swallowed. "Because I fooled myself into believing that I couldn't convince you. That nothing I said would matter. But when I heard Clark calling me by the old nickname he'd tagged me with back in high school, something snapped and I knew I couldn't let you marry him without knowing the truth about him."

Alison looked at her groom. "What old nickname?"

He shook his head. "She's delusional."

"Trailer-park tramp," Dana answered clearly, no longer letting those words hurt her.

The door to the office opened and the best man stepped inside. "The natives are getting restless out there."

"Phil," Alison said, rising, "tell me something."

"What?" he asked. He looked a little perplexed.

Alison licked her dry lips. "Who is the trailer-park tramp?"

Phil's gaze flashed instantly to Dana, then back to Alison again. "I'm not sure what you mean."

"I think you do," Alison said, her voice breaking as Phil ducked back out the door. "I can't believe you would do this to me, Clark. To us."

"So I gave her a stupid nickname in high school," Clark said, still trying to sound reasonable. "That's what she was! She might have everyone else fooled now with her fancy apartment and her designer clothes, but I remember where she came from.''

Alison looked up at him. "You told me you didn't remember her at all.''

Clark faltered, aware he'd been caught in a contradiction. "I didn't…at first. Then it came to me later.''

Her gaze narrowed on him. "I came back from New York on Wednesday and you had a swollen jaw and sore ribs. You told me you got hurt playing basketball at the gym with the guys. But Austin did that to you, didn't he?''

"I was trying to protect you," Clark claimed, spinning wildly now. "Dana did meet me in that hotel suite, but only because she insisted we needed to go over more wedding details. She made a move on me the moment her boyfriend appeared at the door. He got the wrong idea and took it out on me.''

"Austin went there because I called him that morning looking for Dana," Alison explained in a dull, flat voice. "I told him I knew nothing about any meeting.'' She turned to her fiancé. "It's true, isn't it, Clark? Everything she's saying is true.''

"Damn it, Alison.'' He knelt by her feet. "You know what you mean to me. Don't throw it all away for her.''

"I won't.'' Alison sucked in a deep breath. "I'll throw it away for me.''

Clark's jaw dropped, then he stood up and whirled on Dana. "You blew it, lady. I'll make sure your boyfriend rots in jail now.''

Dana refused to let him intimidate her. "If you press charges against Austin, I'll do the same to you.''

"And I'll back her up." Alison lifted her head, tears in her eyes.

"So will I," Father LoBianco said in his quiet, steady voice.

Alison turned to the priest, the tears spilling onto her cheeks. "The wedding is off."

Clark stormed out of the office, the door banging against the wall.

Dana turned to Alison. "I'm so sorry. I should have come to you sooner. I never should have let it all go this far."

"Could you please find my mother?" Alison rasped, her lower lip quivering.

With a nod, Dana followed the priest to the sanctuary, where he announced that the wedding had been indefinitely postponed.

Her heart ached for Alison, but Dana felt an odd sense of empowerment. She'd stood up for herself and done the right thing.

It was a wonderful feeling.

REPORTER DEBBIE NORTH tracked down Dana in the basement of the church twenty minutes later.

"I've been looking all over for you!" Debbie walked into the dressing room and closed the door. "Father LoBianco announced that the wedding is off, but he didn't give any juicy details. What's the scoop?"

Dana gathered the plastic garment bags from the floor. "Well, I'd say my career as a wedding planner is over. Three strikes and you're out."

Debbie cocked her head. "You almost sound happy about it."

"I'm not happy, exactly, just glad that I finally did the right thing before it was too late."

The reporter pulled her tape recorder out of her purse. "Now I definitely smell a story."

"Only if it's off the record," Dana said, taking the recorder out of the woman's hands.

"Hey, you offered me an exclusive on this wedding," Debbie reminded her.

"I won't be talking to any other reporters," Dana promised. "But what I tell you has to stay between us. Alison's been hurt enough already."

"All right," Debbie conceded with a sigh. "I don't kick a bride when she's down. But I am going to ask her for an interview."

"That will be up to her."

Dana took a seat, then motioned for Debbie to do the same. The reporter didn't utter a word the entire time Dana was telling her story.

"Clark Oxley tried to attack you? Twice?" Debbie looked stunned.

Dana nodded. "He got away with it in high school, and I almost let him get away with it again."

"But Austin stopped him the second time. I wish I could have been there to see the fight."

Remembering the horror that had gripped her when Austin went down, Dana closed her eyes. "It was awful."

"Then Oxley blackmails you by threatening the man you love. That is so despicable."

"I never should have agreed to it," Dana said. "What I should have done was told both Austin and Alison the truth immediately. But I let myself believe Clark had more power than I did."

"That's understandable, considering what happened before."

"I was a teenager then," Dana said, not wanting anyone to make excuses for her. "I'm twenty-eight years old now and I should have known better."

"So, what made you stop the wedding today?"

Her throat tightened when she thought about Austin. She didn't think it was possible to miss the man this much. "Because someone recently taught me that no price is too high for honesty and integrity. I guess it finally got through to me."

Dana just wished she had listened to him sooner, before she'd let him walk out of her life.

"What a story," Debbie breathed. "A girl from the wrong side of the tracks brings down a Seattle big shot. There's no way I can sit on this."

"Like I said before, that's up to Alison."

Debbie's eyes lit up. "So if she gives her permission, I can put your words on the record?"

"Sure," Dana conceded, certain Alison would never agree. No doubt the Van Hoek family would want to keep this debacle as quiet as possible.

"But you have to tell me how the story ends," Debbie said.

"You already know. The wedding between Alison Van Hoek and Clark Oxley is off."

"No, I mean how it ends with you and Austin. You're not going to let him keep believing that story Clark made up in that hotel suite, are you?"

Dana's heart yearned to see him again. She couldn't forget the look on Austin's face that day. But she said, "I don't think he'd believe me now."

"But doesn't he deserve to hear the truth?"

"Yes," she admitted, "but I'm not sure I could stand it if he walked away from me again."

"Honesty and integrity are worth any price," Debbie reminded her. "I think you owe it to Austin—and to yourself."

Dana looked up at her, realizing the reporter was right. She couldn't let this lie fester between them any longer. It was time to tell Austin the truth, and deal with the consequences.

"I have to go." Dana grabbed her purse and coat, almost running for the door.

DEBBIE WATCHED HER race out of the dressing room, hoping she'd get a story out of this day before she was through. At least this story seemed to have a beginning, a middle and an end—unlike the twenty-year-old Louis Kinard case that had absorbed her for so many months.

Just this morning she'd been looking at the copious notes and old newspaper clippings that occupied a permanent place on her kitchen table. The story about a murdered priest and a missing antique crystal cross had caught her attention again, because it had happened in this very church.

As she'd sifted through the old newspapers, Debbie had noticed that the story of the church murder and burglary was relegated farther and farther back from the front page in July and August of 1983. Especially after the man arrested for the crimes was acquitted.

She found it very strange that the antique cross had never turned up anywhere. Such a rare relic would be worth a fortune on the black market.

Or had it turned up? Perhaps the newspapers had

missed the story, or she'd simply overlooked it. As she walked out of the dressing room, she thought of one man who might be able to answer her questions.

Debbie wandered the empty church until she finally tracked him down in the stone breezeway that connected the church to the rectory.

"Hello," Father LoBianco said with a smile. "Are you lost?"

"Actually, Father LoBianco, you're just the man I want to see. I'm Debbie North, a reporter for the *Post-Intelligencer.*"

"How nice to meet you, Ms. North," he said, shaking her hand. "But please call me Father Dom."

"Only if you call me Debbie."

"All right, Debbie," he said cordially. "How can I help you?"

Father LoBianco was almost her height, with snow-white hair in a circle around his head that reminded her of the monks of old.

"I've been researching the murder of Father Michael Cleary back in 1983 and the theft of the crystal cross."

He nodded. "Ah, yes. I remember it well. I was serving in another parish at the time, but it sent shock waves through the entire diocese."

"I'm sure it did. Was the relic ever recovered?"

"I'm afraid not. The horrible crime was never solved."

"But they did arrest a man for both the burglary and murder."

"Only on the flimsiest of evidence," Father Dom replied. "I'm sure that's why the jury acquitted him.

No, I'm afraid that case ended up as just one of many of the city's unsolved crimes.''

"Did Father Michael have any enemies that you know of? Anyone who might have killed him?''

"I didn't know him well," Father Dom told her. "But he was not the kind of man to inspire murder. No, I'm certain the perpetrator was after the crystal cross, and poor Father Michael simply got in his way.''

"Surely, if theft was the motive, the cross would have turned up somewhere in the world by now. It's worth a small fortune.''

His brow furrowed. "I've wondered about that myself. Strange, isn't it?''

She nodded, her mind processing all the little clues dangling in front of her. The missing cross. The dead priest. The horrible fire that had killed Louis Kinard's partner, Jonathan Webber, and his wife, Carrie. All unrelated except for the fact that they had occurred on the same hot July night in 1983 in the Queen Anne district of Seattle.

Coincidence? Or was there something more to the story? Something she was still missing.

If so, Debbie was determined to find it.

CHAPTER FOURTEEN

HANNAH SAW THE LAST CHILD out the door at Forrester Square Day Care, so glad that Friday had finally arrived. As happy as she was about her pregnancy, it had zapped her strength. She hoped the prenatal vitamins her obstetrician had prescribed would kick in soon.

Most of the staff were still in their playrooms, taking advantage of the quiet time to organize their materials and prepare for next week. Hannah checked in with each one to get an update on all the children. But as she returned to the first floor from the toddlers' room upstairs, a sudden wave of dizziness overcame her.

She held on to the banister until it passed, wondering why this pregnancy was so different from her first. With Adam, she'd had little nausea or dizziness, though she had been just as tired. Her doctor had told her each pregnancy was unique, and she knew in the end it would all be worth it.

She had so many wonderful things to look forward to. Not only the baby, but her marriage to Jack. Hannah couldn't wait until their wedding day, when the three of them would officially become a family—soon to be four.

Sometimes it still seemed like a miracle that they'd found each other again. The past six months had been a time for miraculous reunions. Like coming together again with her old friends Katherine and Alexandra. Finding Jack and Adam. And Jack reuniting with his younger brother, Austin, after all these years.

Her one regret was that Austin had left Seattle so soon. She knew his abrupt departure had something to do with her wedding planner, but Dana had been so busy lately preparing for the Van Hoek nuptials that Hannah hadn't had a chance to talk with her about it.

Glancing at her watch, she realized the Van Hoek wedding was taking place at this very moment. Hannah hoped it was a smash success, for Dana's sake. Despite the apparent romantic rift with Austin, Hannah truly did see a kindred spirit in Dana Ulrich.

She stopped short outside the closed office door, suddenly aware of the raised voices inside. Her dizziness passed as the voices grew louder. Not wanting to intrude, she stood there with her hand on the doorknob, debating whether to go inside.

Before she could make a decision, the doorknob was wrenched out of her grasp and the door flew open. Griffin Frazier, Alexandra's boyfriend and an officer with the Seattle Police Department, stormed out, almost bumping into Hannah.

"Sorry," Griffin muttered, his mouth tight below his neatly trimmed mustache. She could see both anger and frustration swirling in his brown eyes.

"Are you all right?" Hannah asked, never having seen him this upset before.

"Try to talk some sense into her," Griffin said, then stomped down the hallway and out the door.

Hannah walked into the office and saw Alexandra

pacing the floor, her cheeks flushed and her small body tensely coiled.

"Problems?" Hannah asked gently. "Or is it none of my business?"

Alexandra stopped pacing, though she looked ready to explode. "Griffin's upset with me. He thinks I'm obsessed with Gary Devlin." She threw her hands in the air. "I don't know, maybe I am."

Gary Devlin was a homeless man who had been flushed out of one of the old underground tunnels below the building after a minor fire months ago. Though somewhat confused, he was always gentle, and had befriended Katherine, Hannah and especially Alexandra.

At first, Hannah had thought Alexandra's concern about the man would be a welcome distraction from the horrible nightmares that had been plaguing her recently. That it might help her put her tragic past behind her, once and for all.

Unfortunately, it seemed to be having the opposite effect.

Alexandra sensed something in the homeless man that reminded her of her long-dead father, even though there was no physical resemblance or evidence linking him to the late Jonathan Webber.

That much she'd discovered last month when she'd taken Devlin home for a haircut and a shave to reveal the stranger's face that had been hidden by a full beard and long, straggly hair.

"I don't understand," Hannah said. "Griffin didn't seem to have a problem when he helped you identify Gary Devlin through his fingerprints. Why is he upset now?"

"Because apparently he thought that would be the end of it," Alexandra replied. She slumped into a chair, her nervous energy spent. "I was convinced that Gary was using a false name or had amnesia." She looked up at Hannah. "I was convinced he was my father."

Her heart ached for her friend. "But he looks nothing like him."

"I know," Alexandra admitted, her voice strained. "There's just something about him.... I wish I could explain it. I asked Griffin if he could help me track down Gary's family."

"You think finding his family will help you solve the mystery?" Hannah asked.

"It's the next logical step. I just can't believe no one is looking for him."

"Maybe they've given up. Or don't know where to look."

She nodded. "That's why I believe we should start look for them. I've done some research on the Internet, Hannah. There are hundreds of Devlins in the Pacific Northwest, but there's no way I could possibly contact them all. I thought Griffin might be able to use his resources at the police department to help me narrow the search and find Gary's family."

"And that's when he called you obsessed?"

"Yes." Alexandra met her gaze, her green eyes haunted. "Do you think I am?"

Hannah didn't know what to say. She'd been so caught up in her own life lately, including those puzzling blood tests, that she hadn't spent much time with Alexandra or Katherine. That was going to change.

She walked over and gave her a hug. "No, I think you're wonderful."

Alexandra clung to her for a moment, then pulled away. "Thanks, I needed that."

"I'll help you if I can."

"I wish you could," Alexandra said with a smile. "But I think I need to handle this one on my own."

"Maybe Griffin will come around."

"Maybe," Alexandra conceded, but she didn't sound very hopeful. "He thinks I'm using Gary as a diversion to keep us from getting closer."

"Could he be right?"

Her friend considered the possibility. "I like Griffin and I enjoy dating him. I'm just not sure if I'm ready for more with him or any other man. Not until I figure out why I've been having these disturbing nightmares."

Hannah wished she knew the reason. It seemed to her that Alexandra had suffered more than she deserved. More than anyone deserved.

"Enough of this," Alexandra announced, rising. "We should be talking about happy things, Like your wedding."

"And my baby," Hannah confided.

Alexandra's eyes filled with happy tears. "You're pregnant?"

Hannah nodded. "Looks like we'll need to make room for another crib in the nursery."

"This calls for another hug," Alexandra said, giving her a warm squeeze. "Does Katherine know?"

"Not yet," Hannah replied. "Do you want to tell her?"

Her face lit up like a kid's at Christmas. "Can I?"

Hannah laughed. "Be my guest. She's up in the nursery right now."

Alexandra flew out the door, and Hannah couldn't help but be relieved to see her friend smiling again.

If only she could find a way to make it last.

DANA DROVE STRAIGHT from Our Lady of Mercy to Forrester Square Day Care, hoping Hannah could tell her where to find Austin. She'd finally followed her conscience and now it was time to follow her heart.

Walking through the front door of the day care, she saw Carmen Perez standing in the hallway.

"Well, hello there." Carmen smiled. "I haven't seen you since that trip to the hospital."

"How is Mr. Tidwell?" Dana asked.

"Holding his own." Worry crinkled her brow. "It was touch-and-go for a while, but he's in stable condition now. The doctors can't say how long his recovery will take or if he'll ever recover completely."

"What about Amy?" she asked, remembering the roller-coaster ride of her own emotions when her father fell ill. "How is she holding up?"

"Amy's moved back home with the baby," Carmen said. "She wants to get the house ready for Russ while he's in the hospital and rehab."

"That's a lot of responsibility for a young girl."

Carmen nodded. "I know it won't be easy for her, but she's determined to do what she can. I admire that kind of family loyalty. And I know her boyfriend, Will, does, too, though he's anxious to make the three of them a family of their own. He's agreed to wait until she's ready, though."

"Sounds like Mr. Tidwell is lucky to have her for a daughter."

"Very lucky," Carmen confirmed. "I just hope he realizes it someday."

Dana looked toward the office. "Is Hannah around here somewhere?"

"I saw her earlier today, but I'm not sure if she's still in." Carmen walked over to the office and tapped on the door.

Hannah's voice came from the other side. "Come in."

Carmen winked at Dana. "Looks like you're in luck."

Dana hoped she was right, since she was going to need all the luck she could get. Walking inside the office, she glanced around, surprised to find it empty. Then she noticed a pair of boots on the floor behind the desk and realized they were connected to Hannah.

"Are you all right?" Dana asked, rounding the desk to see the woman lying flat on the carpet. "Do you want me to call Jack?"

"Absolutely not," Hannah said, pulling herself up to a sitting position. "He worries about me enough already. I just got a little dizzy there for a moment and needed to lie down."

"I saw a couch in the nurse's office," Dana said. "I'm sure it's a lot more comfortable than the floor."

"I know," Hannah agreed. "But I'd probably get sidetracked by something on the way upstairs. That's what usually seems to happen. It's just easier to take a five-minute break here on the floor."

"Maybe you're working too hard," Dana suggested.

Hannah laughed. "Now you sound like my fiancé."

"It's my job to make sure the bride is ready to walk down the aisle." *Or walk away.* But Dana wasn't ready to tell Hannah about her latest wedding fiasco.

"I'll be ready," Hannah promised, then placed a hand on her stomach. "I'll also be three months pregnant."

"Austin told me you were expecting. Congratulations."

"Thank you. I just hope I can make it through the ceremony without any problems."

"You'll be fine."

"If I don't faint," Hannah said. "Or throw up. Or grow out of my wedding gown."

"Since you'll only be a few months along, I doubt that will happen. But just in case it does, I have a seamstress on call who can make emergency alterations. I've already had her inspect your gown, and she says expanding the waistline will not be a problem."

Hannah gaped at her as she rose. "Are you serious?"

"Of course. It's my job."

"I think it's more than a job for you, Dana," she mused. "I think you love your work as much as I love mine."

"Guilty as charged," Dana quipped, then sat down on the chair across from the desk. "I can update you on the wedding plans—if this is a good time."

"It's perfect," Hannah assured her, pulling up the desk chair.

"The Harbor Club is reserved for both the ceremony and the reception. I've requested valet parking for the guests, and your father has arranged for several of his friends to offer sailboat rides during the reception."

"I think Adam is more excited about the sailboat rides than the wedding. Although the food comes a close second."

Dana was glad for the reminder. "For the reception we're planning to have a buffet with assorted hors d'oeuvres, both hot and cold. Waiters will also circulate with serving trays."

"Can we have teriyaki chicken wings? I've had the worst craving for teriyaki lately."

"Already done," Dana assured her. "Some barbecue, too, because Austin insisted we include a little bit of Texas in the celebration."

"Jack will be happy to hear it. You can take the cowboy out of Texas, but you can't take Texas out of the cowboy."

"Speaking of Austin," Dana said a little too hastily, "how is he?"

A knowing smile touched Hannah's lips. "As stubborn as ever."

Dana nodded, wondering how to dig further without making it too obvious. But why not? She'd done enough worrying about what other people might think of her to last a lifetime. If Hannah thought she was in love with Austin…well, it was true.

"Is he staying with you?" Dana asked.

"No," Hannah replied. "He went back home."

Her heart dropped to her toes. "To Texas?"

"Back to the Hawke Ranch," Hannah said. "Jack tried to talk him into staying on with us, at least until the wedding, but Austin wouldn't listen. He did promise to come back in April, though, and stand up as Jack's best man."

April? She simply couldn't wait that long.

"So if a girl went to Texas, where exactly would she find the Hawke Ranch?"

Hannah smiled as she pulled a notepad in front of her. "I think I remember it pretty well. I'll draw you a map."

CHAPTER FIFTEEN

AUSTIN STOOD ALONG the fence line, hurtling the post-hole digger into the ground. Digging postholes was one of the most grueling, backbreaking jobs on the ranch. A cool February breeze blew over the land, but he worked with his shirt off, perspiration dripping from every pore.

His new Border collie chased away any barn swallows that dared to land within twenty feet of Austin. He had chosen the runt from a litter of purebreds at a Dallas animal shelter. The dog wasn't much good for chasing cows yet, but at least the Hawke Ranch was safe from small birds.

"C'mon, Dog," Austin said, wiping the sweat off his brow with his forearm. "Let's call it a day."

The Border collie eagerly nipped at the heels of his cowboy boots. Austin knew he had to come up with a name for him, but nothing seemed to fit. A problem that seemed to pervade everything about the ranch lately. He'd been home for almost a week, yet it didn't feel like home anymore. Nothing seemed the same since he'd left Dana behind in Seattle.

He'd walk the floors in the big old house at night, unable to sleep, his footsteps echoing the loneliness he felt in his heart. With each day that passed, he'd drive himself a little harder, trying to work out the frustration that filled him whenever he thought of her.

Which seemed to be every minute of every day.

Austin tossed the posthole digger into the back of his truck, then closed the end gate. Walking around to the driver's door, he reached into the front seat for the shirt he'd discarded earlier. He wadded it up in his hand and wiped away the sweat on his face and chest.

It was dark by the time he pulled into the yard, which was lit only by a mercury light on a pole between the house and the barn. The place didn't look like much yet. The barn was more brown than red, with the paint peeling off the wood. The house looked even worse. It was a three-story colonial, built over a hundred years ago by his great-grandfather. The ranch had been prosperous then. And it would be again.

If he could quit thinking about Dana.

Something just didn't set right with what had happened between them in that hotel suite. How could the passionate woman he'd held in his arms all night long turn to another man the next day? Especially a jerk like Clark Oxley.

"Forget her," Austin muttered aloud as he shifted into park and switched off the engine.

The dog began barking frantically, sighting birds in front of the house. Austin opened the cab door, and the dog jumped over him and landed on the driveway, streaking toward an unsuspecting barn swallow on a tree stump.

At least one of them was happy.

The Border collie circled the drive, ever vigilant, as Austin walked wearily to the mailbox. He pulled open the lid to find a manila envelope among the bills and junk mail.

Turning the envelope over, he saw Jack's name on the return address label. As he walked to the house, he tucked the other mail under his arm, then slipped his thumb under the flap of the large envelope and broke the seal.

What he found inside stopped him in his tracks.

IT TOOK DANA almost a week to drive the two thousand miles from Seattle to Dallas, Texas. The Beast balked at the long trip, breaking down just south of Boise and in the mountains outside of Denver. The car repairs drained what was left of her bank account, and in the end, it would have been cheaper for her to fly to Texas.

But Dana put those frustrations behind her as she drove up the gravel road leading to the Hawke Ranch. She had Hannah's hand-drawn map spread out on the steering wheel in front of her as she tried to make out the directions in the growing darkness.

She hadn't met any other traffic for the past ten miles, though she'd seen plenty of cows and even a roadrunner or two. Her stomach began to flutter when she made the final turn. Would Austin be happy to find her here, or would he order her off his ranch?

If nothing else, she had to make him listen to her story. He had to know the truth. Austin deserved at least that much from her.

And the truth was that she was crazy in love with him.

Dana slammed on the brakes, realizing she'd just driven past the long driveway. There was no sign heralding the Hawke Ranch, but according to the wrinkled map in front of her, this was the place. The Beast skidded on the loose gravel, then bucked to a stop. She shifted into reverse, but when she pushed on the gas pedal the engine sputtered and died.

"Great," she muttered, pumping the pedal before attempting to start it again. But nothing happened. The Beast wasn't going anywhere.

Climbing out of the car, she closed the door behind her, then headed for the driveway. The evening air smelled like rain with a faint hint of clover. As the sun set on the horizon, it cast a pastel palette of pink, blue and purple over the cloudy sky.

She could see the silhouette of a big house behind a stand of willow trees, and a towering red barn beyond it. Her breath caught at the beauty of the scene in the fading twilight. But what she noticed most of all was the calming silence surrounding her. No car horns or sirens. No planes flying overhead or boom boxes blaring. Just the gentle chirp of a cricket and the soft rustle of dry grass in the fields.

A few stars glittered in the sky as day surrendered to night.

As Dana drew nearer to the house, Austin's shiny red pickup suddenly came into view, parked on the edge of the front lawn.

He was home.

If the rapid thud of her heart didn't announce her arrival, the shrill barking of his dog surely would. She saw the small black-and-white Border collie catapult through the open barn doors and race toward her, stopping only long enough to mark its territory on a small tree stump. When the dog reached her, it sniffed her shoes, then growled low in its throat.

"Nice puppy," she said, bending down to cautiously pet its furry white head.

It growled again, a low, menacing warning.

"Dog!"

The sound of Austin's voice made her jump. The dog jumped too, then streaked toward its master. Dana slowly straightened, watching Austin walk toward her.

She could tell the instant he recognized her. His step faltered for a moment, then his eyes narrowed. But he kept walking. That was a good sign.

She held her breath as he approached, wondering what he was thinking. Maybe Austin would admire her for coming this far to see him. Maybe he wouldn't give her a chance to say one word.

Let him try, she thought to herself, lifting her chin as he stopped in front of her. She wasn't going anywhere until she told him what she'd traveled over two thousand miles to say.

Austin didn't try to do anything. He just stood there, his gray eyes boring into her.

Unnerved by his silence, at last she said, "His name is Dog?"

Austin glanced down at the black-and-white fur ball at his feet, then back at Dana again. "For now."

So much for pleasantries. She licked her dry lips. "I have something to say and I want you to listen."

He folded his arms across his chest. "Is that right?"

She nodded. "That's right. I know you can be stubborn and hardheaded and…"

He moved closer, making the words die on her lips.

''Is that what you came all the way from Seattle to tell me? Because if it is...''

''No,'' she said. ''I came here to tell you that I love you.''

Dana had meant to save that part for last, but she had wanted to say it to him for so long that it just slipped out. Now she had to keep talking before she ran out of nerve.

''I lied that day in the hotel suite,'' she continued, searching his face for some reaction. ''I thought I was protecting you, but now I know it was more than that. I was protecting myself from being called a liar again. Not by you,'' she added hastily. ''I knew you would believe me.''

His gaze softened. ''Is that right?''

A smile twitched at her lips. ''Yes. Because if you had let me finish before, you'd know that I think you're stubborn and hardheaded and loyal to the core. You believe in truth. You believe in me.''

''You forgot one thing,'' Austin said, taking another step closer.

She'd forgotten how much taller he was than her. How intimidating his size could be. ''What?''

''You forgot that I love you.''

''You do?'' she asked, her voice cracking with the hope she'd battered down since he'd left her in Seattle. Now it sprang forth inside her, filling her with warmth.

''Always,'' he replied, pulling her to him. He captured her mouth in a passionate kiss, one rough hand cradling her cheek.

Dana closed her eyes and wrapped her arms around his neck, sinking into his hard body. Feeling as if she'd finally come home.

A loud bark broke them apart at last, the dog twisting himself between their legs.

"I think he's lonely," Dana said, laughing.

"I know the feeling," Austin replied huskily.

She looked into his gray eyes, now shining with love for her. "This seems too easy. I had a big speech planned out. All my points and counterpoints on why you should give me another chance."

"Go ahead," he teased. "I'll listen."

She took a deep breath. "I stopped the Van Hoek wedding."

"I know."

Her eyes widened. "But how?"

"My brother sent me a newspaper article that told all about it. Sounds like you're going to be the most popular wedding planner in Seattle."

"I am?" she said, puzzled. Another botched wedding should have snapped the final thread holding together her tattered career. What newspaper article had predicted the opposite?

Then it occurred to her that she'd left the morning after the botched wedding and had been on the road for a week, so she hadn't seen any Seattle papers. Had Alison really given her consent for an interview, or had Debbie North printed her off-the-record version?

"Don't look so worried," Austin said. "It made you look good. Alison sung your praises to the sky, and that reporter made you look like the guardian angel of brides everywhere. Best of all, good old Clark can forget about a political career. By the time I was through reading the article, I almost felt sorry for the guy. He's burned toast in that town."

She laughed. "Really?"

"Okay, I lied. I didn't feel sorry for him."

"I thought Austin Hawke *never* lied," she teased.

"Only to myself," he said softly, "when I thought I could live without you."

"I won't let you," she promised, leaning up to kiss him again. His arms tightened around her as his mouth molded over hers. Their kiss was deep. Tender. Yearning.

The dog whined at their feet.

Austin broke off the kiss, glaring at the dog. "Never interrupt a cowboy when he's courting a lady. Especially a city girl. They scare easy."

"Not anymore," Dana promised him.

He brushed a stray curl off her cheek. "I suppose you'll be fielding job offers left and right when we go back to Seattle."

"My career is definitely headed in a new direction," she replied. "But I'm going to land the wedding of my dreams right here in Texas."

"Whose wedding is that?"

"Mine."

He grinned. "Please tell me I'm the lucky groom."

"The luckiest. You get to bring a city girl home to the ranch."

Surprise lit his face. "You want to live here?"

She smiled. "I think I'll like it, Austin. Our life will be like *Green Acres,* but with a nicer house."

He glanced at the large ramshackle home behind him. "Not much nicer."

"Remember what you told me in Seattle?" she asked him. "Life is about how you live, not how you look."

"I was wrong," he said huskily. "Life is about how you love." Then he kissed her long and deep.

"I love you," Dana murmured against his mouth.

His lips nibbled their way down her neck. "And I love you, city girl."

"I may be a city girl, but I'm not afraid of hard work." She shifted in his embrace to gaze at the house they would share together.

"A little paint," she mused, "some landscaping, a fountain and a gazebo or two and this place will be beautiful. In fact, I think I could launch my new wedding planner business from right here. I just read in *Bride Magazine* that country weddings are all the rage."

"Then, let's get started," he said, scooping her up into his arms.

"Where are you taking me?"

"To the hardware store to buy paint. I'm thinking white for the house and blue for the shutters."

"Just like my old home," she said wistfully. But Dana didn't need a certain house to make her happy anymore. Just a certain man.

She leaned against his broad chest as he carried her toward his truck, a little disappointed that Austin didn't want to ravish her after their being apart for so long.

"How far is it to the hardware store?"

"The nearest town is only about five miles away. But we have to take the detour, so we won't get there for several hours."

"Several hours?" she echoed. "What kind of detour is that?"

He grinned as he carried her past his truck and

straight toward the house. "The best kind. It goes right through my bedroom."

She grabbed his hat off his head and placed it on her own. "I like the way you think, cowboy."

"Ma'am, just wait until you see what else I can do."

* * * * *

FORRESTER SQUARE,
a new Harlequin series,
continues in February 2004 with
TOO GOOD TO REFUSE
by Mindy Neff...

*Millie Gallagher was barely an adult when
her parents died and she took on the role of
"mom" to her baby sister, Lindsey. That was
four years ago. Millie gave up her dream of
college, worked three jobs—but never
regretted her choice. Now her life's about to
take a fairy-tale turn. She's been hired as a
temporary nanny...by a sheikh!*

Here's a preview!

CHAPTER ONE

"HI." MILLIE SMILED to cover her nervousness and to put the security guard at ease. He probably had a gun under that jacket, and she didn't want him using it on her. What in the world had Katherine gotten her into?

"I'm Millie Gallagher, the new nanny. And this is Lindsey. I believe Mr. Kareem is expecting us…?" She laughed, and a robin flew from the juniper tree. "That was pretty silly. Of course he's expecting us. He sent that gorgeous boat to pick us up. Did you know it was teak on the floors and marble in the bathrooms? That thing's furnished better than most homes. And…I'm talking too much. It's a curse, but what can you do? It's my first day—which you probably know."

The man's shoulders relaxed, and he nodded. "My name is Sadiq. You may call me Deke if you wish."

Millie stuck out her hand. "I'm pleased to meet you, Deke. Should we just go on in, or what?"

"Yes. You are expected." He unlocked the front gate and held it for her.

She noticed that he smelled faintly of peppermint, as though he'd just bitten into a hard candy.

"I will give you a full briefing on security and the layout of the island, once you are settled in."

Security briefing? On a private island?

She and Lindsey walked through a courtyard that easily could have become an overgrown mess if some clever landscaper hadn't been so meticulous in its design. Hints of color sprouted amid exotic greenery draped in pots and beds and even in a whimsical statuary frog. A cherub fountain splashed water in a serene flow over tiers of stone. The entrance smelled like a flourishing nursery, all damp earth, cool shade and wet stone.

At the double-door entry to the house, Millie pressed the button beneath an intercom box, and smiled down at Lindsey as the doorbell chimed eight notes.

The door swung open. She'd expected a butler or a maid, but...

Oh...my...gosh.

For an endless moment she stood paralyzed, stunned.

Scowling down at her was the incredibly virile, deliciously gorgeous, surly man she'd had the misfortune to encounter at the Space Needle.

Peachy.

Good thing she hadn't burned any bridges with her old boss.

"Mr. Kareem, I presume?" she asked when she found the wherewithal to unstick her jaw.

"*Al*-Kareem," he corrected. "Sheikh Jeffri al-Kareem from Balriyad. And how did you find my home?" he demanded.

Sheikh? *Oh, Katherine, you are toast.*

LEGACIES . LIES . LOVE .

Collect four (4) original proofs of purchase from the back pages of the four (4) Forrester Square titles listed below and receive a beautiful picture frame valued at over $20.00 U.S.!

WORD OF HONOR by Dani Sinclair,
on-sale January 2004 (0-373-61273-7)

THIRD TIME'S THE CHARM by Kristin Gabriel,
on-sale February 2004 (0-373-61274-5)

TOO GOOD TO REFUSE by Mindy Neff,
on-sale March 2004 (0-373-61275-3)

ILLEGALLY YOURS by Jacqueline Diamond,
on-sale April 2004 (0-373-61276-1)

Just complete the order form and send it, along with the four (4) proofs of purchase from these four (4) different Forrester Square titles, to: Forrester Square, P.O. Box 9057, Buffalo, NY 14269-9057, or P.O. Box 622, Fort Erie, Ontario L2A 5X3.

Name (PLEASE PRINT)

Address   Apt. #

City   State/Prov.   Zip/Postal Code

098 KJR DXHR

Enclosed are my four (4) proofs of purchase. Please send me my picture frame.

Have you enclosed your proofs of purchase?

One Proof Of Purchase
FSQPOP2

Please allow 4-6 weeks for delivery. Shipping and handling included. Offer good only while quantities last. Offer limited to one (1) per household. Offer available in Canada and the U.S. only. Request should be received no later than **October 18, 2004.** All four (4) proofs of purchase should be cut out of the back-page ads featuring this offer.

© 2003 Harlequin Enterprises Limited

Visit us at www.eHarlequin.com   FSQPOP2

LEGACIES . LIES . LOVE .

If you missed any of the previous riveting stories from Forrester Square, here's a chance to order your copies today!

0-373-61268-0	REINVENTING JULIA by Muriel Jensen	___ $4.99 U.S. ___ $5.99 CAN.
0-373-61269-9	TWICE AND FOR ALWAYS by Cathy Gillen Thacker	___ $4.99 U.S. ___ $5.99 CAN.
0-373-61270-2	ALL SHE NEEDED by Kate Hoffmann	___ $4.99 U.S. ___ $5.99 CAN.
0-373-61271-0	RING OF DECEPTION by Sandra Marton	___ $4.99 U.S. ___ $5.99 CAN.
0-373-61272-9	KEEPING FAITH by Day Leclaire	___ $4.99 U.S. ___ $5.99 CAN.
0-373-61273-7	WORD OF HONOR by Dani Sinclair	___ $4.99 U.S. ___ $5.99 CAN.

(limited quantities available)

TOTAL AMOUNT	$_____
POSTAGE & HANDLING	$_____
($1.00 for one book; 50¢ for each additional)	
APPLICABLE TAXES*	$_____
TOTAL PAYABLE	$_____

(Check or money order—please do not send cash)

To order, send the completed form, along with a check or money order for the total above, payable to **Forrester Square,** to:

In the U.S.: 3010 Walden Avenue, P.O. Box 9077, Buffalo, NY 14269-9077;
In Canada: P.O. Box 636, Fort Erie, Ontario L2A 5X3

Name:_____

Address:_____ City:_____

State/Prov.:_____ Zip/Postal Code:_____

Account # (if applicable):_____

*New York residents remit applicable sales taxes.
*Canadian residents remit applicable GST and provincial taxes.

075 CSAS

If you enjoyed what you just read,
then we've got an offer you can't resist!

Take 2
bestselling novels FREE!
Plus get a FREE surprise gift!

Clip this page and mail it to The Best of the Best™

IN U.S.A.	**IN CANADA**
3010 Walden Ave.	P.O. Box 609
P.O. Box 1867	Fort Erie, Ontario
Buffalo, N.Y. 14240-1867	L2A 5X3

YES! Please send me 2 free Best of the Best™ novels and my free surprise gift. After receiving them, if I don't wish to receive anymore, I can return the shipping statement marked cancel. If I don't cancel, I will receive 4 brand-new novels every month, before they're available in stores! In the U.S.A., bill me at the bargain price of $4.74 plus 25¢ shipping and handling per book and applicable sales tax, if any*. In Canada, bill me at the bargain price of $5.24 plus 25¢ shipping and handling per book and applicable taxes**. That's the complete price and a savings of over 20% off the cover prices—what a great deal! I understand that accepting the 2 free books and gift places me under no obligation ever to buy any books. I can always return a shipment and cancel at any time. Even if I never buy another The Best of the Best™ book, the 2 free books and gift are mine to keep forever.

185 MDN DNWF
385 MDN DNWG

Name	(PLEASE PRINT)	
Address	Apt.#	
City	State/Prov.	Zip/Postal Code

* Terms and prices subject to change without notice. Sales tax applicable in N.Y.
** Canadian residents will be charged applicable provincial taxes and GST.
  All orders subject to approval. Offer limited to one per household and not valid to
  current The Best of the Best™ subscribers.
® are registered trademarks of Harlequin Enterprises Limited.

BOB02-R   ©1998 Harlequin Enterprises Limited